English Men of Letters

EDITED BY JOHN MORLEY

BURKE

BY

JOHN MORLEY

NEW YORK

HARPER & BROTHERS, PUBLISHERS

FRANKLIN SQUARE

ENGLISH MEN OF LETTERS.

EDITED BY JOHN MORLEY.

12mo, Cloth, 75 cents per volume.

PUBLISHED BY HARPER & BROTHERS, NEW YORK.

☞ *Any of the above works will be sent by mail, postage prepaid, to any part of the United States, on receipt of the price.*

NOTE.

THE present writer published a study on Burke some
twelve years ago. It was almost entirely critical, and in
no sense a narrative. The volume now submitted to the
readers of this Series is biographical rather than critical,
and not more than about a score of pages have been re-
produced in it from the earlier book. Three pages (pp.
211–213) have been inserted from an article on Burke
contributed by me to the new edition of the *Encyclopædia
Britannica;* and I have to thank Messrs. Black for the
great courtesy with which they have allowed me to tran-
scribe the passage here. These borrowings from my former self, the reader will perhaps be willing to excuse, on
the old Greek principle, that a man may once say a thing
as he would have it said, δὶς δὲ οὐκ ἐνδέχεται—he cannot
say it twice.

J. M.

CONTENTS.

CONTENTS.

CHAPTER VIII.

CHAPTER IX.

CHAPTER X.

BURKE.

CHAPTER I.

EARLY LIFE, AND FIRST WRITINGS.

It will soon be a hundred and twenty years since Burke first took his seat in the House of Commons, and it is eighty-five years since his voice ceased to be heard there. Since his death, as during his life, opinion as to the place to which he is entitled among the eminent men of his country has touched every extreme. Tories have extolled him as the saviour of Europe. Whigs have detested him as the destroyer of his party. One undiscriminating pan-egyrist calls him the most profound and comprehensive of political philosophers that has yet existed in the world. Another and more distinguished writer insists that he is a resplendent and far-seeing rhetorician, rather than a deep and subtle thinker. A third tells us that his works can-not be too much our study, if we mean either to under-stand or to maintain against its various enemies, open and concealed, designing and mistaken, the singular constitu-tion of this fortunate island. A fourth, on the contrary, declares that it would be hard to find a single leading principle or prevailing sentiment in one half of these works, to which something extremely adverse cannot be

1*

found in the other half. A fifth calls him one of the
greatest men, and, Bacon alone excepted, the greatest
thinker, who ever devoted himself to the practice of English politics. Yet, oddly enough, the author of the fifth
verdict will have it that this great man and great thinker was actually out of his mind, when he composed the
pieces for which he has been most widely admired and
revered.

A sufficient interval has now passed to allow all the sed-
iment of party fanaticism to fall to the bottom. The circumstances of the world have since Burke's time undergone variation enough to enable us to judge, from many
points of view, how far he was the splendid pamphleteer
of a faction, and how far he was a contributor to the universal stock of enduring wisdom. Opinion is slowly, but
without reaction, settling down to the verdict that Burke
is one of the abiding names in our history, not because he
either saved Europe or destroyed the Whig party; but because he added to the permanent considerations of wise
political thought, and to the maxims of wise practice in
great affairs, and because he imprints himself upon us with
a magnificence and elevation of expression, that places him
among the highest masters of literature, in one of its highest and most commanding senses. Those who have acquired a love for abstract politics amid the almost mathe-
matical closeness and precision of Hobbes, the philosophic
calm of Locke or Mill, or even the majestic and solemn
fervour of Milton, are revolted by the unrestrained passion
and the decorated style of Burke. His passion appears
hopelessly fatal to success in the pursuit of Truth, who
does not usually reveal herself to followers thus inflamed.
His ornate style appears fatal to the cautious and precise method of statement, suitable to matter which is not

known at all unless it is known distinctly. Yet the natural ardour which impelled Burke to clothe his judgments
in glowing and exaggerated phrases, is one secret of his
power over us, because it kindles in those who are capable
of that generous infection a respondent interest and sympathy. But more than this, the reader is speedily conscious of the precedence in Burke of the facts of morality
and conduct, of the many interwoven affinities of human
affection and historical relation, over the unreal necessi-
ties of mere abstract logic. Burke's mind was full of the
matter of great truths, copiously enriched from the foun-
tains of generous and many-coloured feeling. He thought
about life as a whole, with all its infirmities and all its
pomps. With none of the mental exclusiveness of the
moralist by profession, he fills every page with solemn reference and meaning; with none of the mechanical bustle
of the common politician, he is everywhere conscious of
the mastery of laws, institutions, and government over the
character and happiness of men. Besides thus diffusing a
strong light over the awful tides of human circumstance,
Burke has the sacred gift of inspiring men to use a grave
diligence in caring for high things, and in making their
lives at once rich and austere. Such a part in literature is
indeed high. We feel no emotion of revolt when Mackintosh speaks of Shakespere and Burke in the same breath,
as being both of them above mere talent. And we do not
dissent when Macaulay, after reading Burke's works over
again, exclaims, "How admirable! The greatest man since
Milton!"

The precise date of Burke's birth cannot be stated with
certainty. All that we can say is that it took place either
in 1728 or 1729, and it is possible that we may set it

down in one or the other year, as we choose to reckon by
the old or the new style. The best opinion is that he
was born at Dublin on the 12th of January, 1729 (N.S.).
His father was a solicitor in good practice, and is believed
to have been descended from some Bourkes of county
Limerick, who held a respectable local position in the time
of the civil wars. Burke's mother belonged to the Nagle
family, which had a strong connexion in the county of
Cork; they had been among the last adherents of James
II., and they remained firm Catholics. Mrs. Burke remained true to the church of her ancestors, and her only
daughter was brought up in the same faith. Edmund
Burke and his two brothers, Garret and Richard, were
bred in the religion of their father; but Burke never, in
after-times, lost a large and generous way of thinking
about the more ancient creed of his mother and his uncles.
In 1741 he was sent to school at Ballitore, a village
some thirty miles away from Dublin, where Abraham
Shackleton, a Quaker from Yorkshire, had established himself fifteen years before, and had earned a wide reputation
as a successful teacher and a good man. According to
Burke, he richly deserved this high character. It was to
Abraham Shackleton that he always professed to owe
whatever gain had come to him from education. If I am
anything, he said many years afterwards, it is the education
I had there that has made me so. His master's skill as a
teacher did not impress him more than the example which
was every day set before him of uprightness and simplicity of heart. Thirty years later, when Burke had the news
of Shackleton's death (1771), "I had a true honour and
affection," he wrote, "for that excellent man. I feel
something like a satisfaction in the midst of my concern,
that I was fortunate enough to have him once under my

roof before his departure." No man has ever had a deeper or more tender reverence than Burke for homely goodness, simple purity, and all the pieties of life; it may well be that this natural predisposition of all characters at once so genial and so serious as his, was finally stamped in him by his first schoolmaster. It is true that he was only two years at Ballitore, but two years at that plastic time often build up habits in the mind that all the rest of a life is unable to pull down.

In 1743 Burke became a student of Trinity College, Dublin, and he remained there until 1748, when he took his Bachelor's degree. These five years do not appear to have been spent in strenuous industry in the beaten paths of academic routine. Like so many other men of great gifts, Burke in his youth was desultory and excursive. He roamed at large over the varied heights that tempt our curiosity, as the dawn of intelligence first lights them up one after another with bewitching visions and illusive magic. "All my studies," Burke wrote in 1746, when he was in the midst of them, "have rather proceeded from sallies of passion, than from the preference of sound reason; and, like all other natural appetites, have been very violent for a season, and very soon cooled, and quite absorbed in the succeeding. I have often thought it a humorous consideration to observe and sum up all the madness of this kind I have fallen into this two years past. First, I was greatly taken with natural philosophy; which, while I should have given my mind to logic, employed me incessantly. This I call my *furor mathematicus*. But this worked off as soon as I began to read it in the college, as men by repletion cast off their stomachs all they have eaten. Then I turned back to logic and metaphysics. Here I remained a good while, and with much pleasure, and this was my *furor logi-*

cus, a disease very common in the days of ignorance, and very uncommon in these enlightened times. Next succeeded the *furor historicus*, which also had its day, but is now no more, being entirely absorbed in the *furor poeticus*."

This is from one of Burke's letters to Richard Shackleton, the son of his schoolmaster, with whom he had formed one of those close friendships that fill the life of generous youth, as ambition fills an energetic manhood. Many tears were shed when the two boys parted at Ballitore, and they kept up their intimacy by a steady correspondence. They discuss the everlasting dispute as to the ultimate fate of those who never heard the saving name of Christ. They send one another copies of verses, and Burke prays for Shackleton's judgment on an invocation of his new poem, to beauteous nymphs who haunt the dusky wood, which hangs recumbent o'er the crystal flood. Burke is warned by Shackleton to endeavour to live according to the rules of the Gospel, and he humbly accepts the good advice, with the deprecatory plea that in a town it is difficult to sit down to think seriously : it is easier, he says, to follow the rules of the Gospel in the country, than at Trinity College, Dublin. In the region of profaner things the two friends canvass the comparative worth of Sallust and of Tully's Epistles. Burke holds for the historian, who has, he thinks, a fine, easy, diversified narrative, mixed with reflection, moral and political, neither very trite nor obvious, nor out of the way and abstract, and this is the true beauty of historical observation.

Some pages of verse describe to Shackleton how his friend passes the day, but the reader will perhaps be content to learn in humbler prose that Burke rose with the dawn, and strode forth into the country through fragrant

gardens and the pride of May, until want of breakfast
drove him back unwillingly to the town, where amid lectures and books his heart incessantly turned to the river
and the fir woods of Ballitore. In the evening he again
turned his back on the city, taking his way " where Liffey
rolls her dead dogs to the sea," along to the wall on the
shore, whence he delighted to see the sun sink into the
waters, gilding ocean, ships, and city as it vanished.
Alas, it was beneath the dignity of verse to tell us what
we should most gladly have known. For,

> " The muse nor can, nor will declare,
> 　What is my work, and what my studies there."

What serious nourishment Burke was laying in for his
understanding, we cannot learn from any other source.
He describes himself as spending three hours almost every
day in the public library. " The best way in the world,"
he adds oddly enough, " of killing thought." I have
read some history, he says, and among other pieces of
history, " I am endeavouring to get a little into the accounts of this, our own poor country " — a pathetic expression, which represents Burke's perpetual mood, as long
as he lived, of affectionate pity for his native land. Of
the eminent Irishmen whose names adorn the annals of
Trinity College in the eighteenth century, Burke was only
contemporary at the University with one, the luckless
sizar who in the fulness of time wrote the *Vicar of Wakefield*. There is no evidence that at this time he and Goldsmith were acquainted with one another. Flood had gone
to Oxford some time before. The one or two companions
whom Burke mentions in his letters are only shadows of
names. The mighty Swift died in 1745, but there is
nothing of Burke's upon the event. In the same year

came the Pretender's invasion, and Burke spoke of those
who had taken part in it in the same generous spirit
that he always showed to the partisans of lost historic
causes.

Of his own family Burke says little, save that in 1746
his mother had a dangerous illness. In all my life, he
writes to his friend, I never found so heavy a grief, nor
really did I well know what it was before. Burke's father
is said to have been a man of angry and irritable temper,
and their disagreements were frequent. This unhappy
circumstance made the time for parting not unwelcome.
In 1747 Burke's name had been entered at the Middle
Temple, and after taking his degree, he prepared to go
to England to pursue the ordinary course of a lawyer's
studies. He arrived in London in the early part of
1750.

A period of nine years followed, in which the circumstances of Burke's life are enveloped in nearly complete
obscurity. He seems to have kept his terms in the regular way at the Temple, and from the mastery of legal principles and methods which he afterwards showed in some
important transactions, we might infer that he did more
to qualify himself for practice than merely dine in the
hall of his Inn. For law, alike as a profession and an instrument of mental discipline, he had always the profound
respect that it so amply deserves, though he saw that it
was not without drawbacks of its own. The law, he
said, in his fine description of George Grenville, in words
that all who think about schemes of education ought to
ponder, " is, in my opinion, one of the first and noblest
of human sciences ; *a science which does more to quicken
and invigorate the understanding than all the other kinds
of learning put together ;* but it is not apt, except in

persons very happily born, to open and to liberalize the mind exactly in the same proportion."[1] Burke was never called to the bar, and the circumstance that, about the time when he ought to have been looking for his first guinea, he published a couple of books which had as little as possible to do with either law or equity, is a tolerably sure sign that he had followed the same desultory courses at the Temple as he had followed at Trinity College. We have only to tell over again a very old story. The vague attractions of literature prevailed over the duty of taking up a serious profession. His father, who had set his heart on having a son in the rank of a barrister, was first suspicious, then extremely indignant, and at last he withdrew his son's allowance, or else reduced it so low that the recipient could not possibly live upon it. This catastrophe took place some time in 1755 —a year of note in the history of literature, as the date of the publication of Johnson's Dictionary. It was upon literature, the most seductive, the most deceiving, the most dangerous of professions, that Burke, like so many hundreds of smaller men before and since, now threw himself for a livelihood.

Of the details of the struggle we know very little. Burke was not fond in after-life of talking about his earlier days, not because he had any false shame about the straits and hard shifts of youthful neediness, but because he was endowed with a certain inborn stateliness of nature, which made him unwilling to waste thoughts on the less dignified parts of life. This is no unqualified virtue, and Burke might have escaped some wearisome frets and embarrassments in his existence, if he had been capable of letting the detail of the day lie more heavily upon him.

[1] *American Taxation.*

So far as it goes, however, it is a sign of mental health
that a man should be able to cast behind him the barren
memories of bye-gone squalor. We may be sure that
whatever were the external ordeals of his apprenticeship
in the slippery craft of the literary adventurer, Burke never failed in keeping for his constant companions generous
ambitions and high thoughts. He appears to have fre-
quented the debating clubs in Fleet Street and the Piazza
of Covent Garden, and he showed the common taste of
his time for the theatre. He was much of a wanderer,
partly from the natural desire of restless youth to see the
world, and partly because his health was weak. In after-
life he was a man of great strength, capable not only of
bearing the strain of prolonged application to books and
papers in the solitude of his library, but of bearing it at
the same time with the distracting combination of active
business among men. At the date of which we are speaking, he used to seek a milder air at Bristol, or in Mon-
mouthshire, or Wiltshire. He passed the summer in retired country villages, reading and writing with desultory
industry, in company with William Burke, a namesake but
perhaps no kinsman. It would be interesting to know
the plan and scope of his studies. We are practically reduced to conjecture. In a letter of counsel to his son in
after-years, he gave him a weighty piece of advice, which
is pretty plainly the key to the reality and fruitfulness of
his own knowledge. "*Redding*," he said, " *and much
reading is good. But the power of diversifying the matter
infinitely in your own mind, and of applying it to every
occasion that arises, is far better; so don't suppress the* vi-
vida vis." We have no more of Burke's doings than obscure and tantalizing glimpses, tantalizing, because he was
then at the age when character usually either fritters itself

away, or grows strong on the inward sustenance of solid
and resolute aspirations. Writing from Battersea to his
old comrade, Shackleton, in 1757, he begins with an apology for a long silence which seems to have continued from
months to years. "I have broken all rules; I have neglected all decorums; everything except that I have never
forgot a friend, whose good head and heart have made me
esteem and love him. What appearance there may have
been of neglect, arises from my manner of life; chequered
with various designs; sometimes in London, sometimes in
remote parts of the country; sometimes in France, and
shortly, please God, to be in America."

One of the hundred inscrutable rumours that hovered
about Burke's name was, that he at one time actually did
visit America. This was just as untrue as that he became
a convert to the Catholic faith; or that he was the lover
of Peg Woffington; or that he contested Adam Smith's
chair of moral philosophy at Glasgow along with Hume,
and that both Burke and Hume were rejected in favour
of some fortunate Mr. James Clow. They are all alike
unfounded. But the same letter informs Shackleton of
a circumstance more real and more important than any
of these, though its details are only doubtfully known.
Burke had married — when and where, we cannot tell.
Probably the marriage took place in the winter of 1756.
His wife was the daughter of Dr. Nugent, an Irish physician once settled at Bath. One story is that Burke consulted him in one of his visits to the west of England, and
fell in love with his daughter. Another version makes
Burke consult him after Dr. Nugent had removed to London; and tells how the kindly physician, considering that
the noise and bustle of chambers over a shop must hinder
his patient's recovery, offered him rooms in his own house.

However these things may have been, all the evidence
shows Burke to have been fortunate in the choice or accident that bestowed upon him his wife. Mrs. Burke, like
her father, was, up to the time of her marriage, a Catholic.
Good judges belonging to her own sex describe her as
gentle, quiet, soft in her manners, and well-bred. She had
the qualities which best fitted and disposed her to soothe
the vehemence and irritability of her companion. Though
she afterwards conformed to the religion of her husband,
it was no insignificant coincidence that in two of the dear-
est relations of his life the atmosphere of Catholicism was
thus poured round the great preacher of the crusade
against the Revolution.

About the time of his marriage, Burke made his first
appearance as an author. It was in 1756 that he published *A Vindication of Natural Society*, and the more
important essay, *A Philosophical Inquiry into the Origin
of our Ideas on the Sublime and Beautiful*. The latter of
them had certainly been written a long time before, and
there is even a traditional legend that Burke wrote it when
he was only nineteen years old. Both of these performances have in different degrees a historic meaning, but
neither of them would have survived to our own day unless they had been associated with a name of power. A
few words will suffice to do justice to them here. And
first as to the *Vindication of Natural Society*. Its alternative title was, *A View of the Miseries and Evils arising to
Mankind from every Species of Civil Society, in a Letter
to Lord ——, by a late Noble Writer*. Bolingbroke had
died in 1751, and in 1754 his philosophical works were
posthumously given to the world by David Mallet, Dr.
Johnson's beggarly Scotchman, to whom Bolingbroke had
left half-a-crown in his will, for firing off a blunderbuss

which he was afraid to fire off himself. The world of letters had been keenly excited about Bolingbroke. His busy and chequered career, his friendship with the great wits of the previous generation, his splendid style, his bold opinions, made him a dazzling figure. This was the late Noble Writer whose opinions Burke intended to ridicule, by reducing them to an absurdity in an exaggeration of Bolingbroke's own manner. As it happened, the public did not readily perceive either the exaggeration in the manner, or the satire in the matter. Excellent judges of style made sure that the writing was really Bolingbroke's, and serious critics of philosophy never doubted that the writer, whoever he was, meant all that he said. We can hardly help agreeing with Godwin, when he says that in Burke's treatise the evils of existing political institutions, which had been described by Locke, are set forth more at large, with incomparable force of reasoning and lustre of eloquence, though the declared intention of the writer was to show that such evils ought to be considered merely trivial. Years afterwards, Boswell asked Johnson whether an imprudent publication by a certain friend of his at an early period of his life, would be likely to hurt him? "No, sir," replied the sage; "not much; it might perhaps be mentioned at an election." It is significant that in 1765, when Burke saw his chance of a seat in Parliament, he thought it worth while to print a second edition of his *Vindication*, with a preface to assure his readers that the design of it was ironical. It has been remarked as a very extraordinary circumstance that an author who had the greatest fame of any man of his day as the master of a superb style, for this was indeed Bolingbroke's position, should have been imitated to such perfection by a mere novice, that accomplished critics like Chesterfield and War-

burton should have mistaken the copy for a first-rate original.   It is, however, to be remembered that the very bold-
ness and sweeping rapidity of Bolingbroke's prose rendered it more fit for imitation, than if its merits had been
those of delicacy or subtlety ; and we must remember that
the imitator was no pygmy, but himself one of the giants.
What is certain is that the study of Bolingbroke which
preceded this excellent imitation left a permanent mark,
and traces of Bolingbroke were never effaced from the
style of Burke.

The point of the *Vindication* is simple enough.   It is
to show that the same instruments which Bolingbroke had
employed in favour of natural against revealed religion,
could be employed with equal success in favour of natural
as against, what Burke calls, artificial society.   " Show
me," cries the writer, " an absurdity in religion, and I will
undertake to show you a hundred for one in political laws
and institutions. . . . If, after all, you should confess all
these things yet plead the necessity of political institutions,
weak and wicked as they are, I can argue with equal, perhaps superior force, concerning the necessity of artificial religion ; and every step you advance in your argument, you
add a strength to mine.   So that, if we are resolved to submit our reason and our liberty to civil usurpation, we have
nothing to do but to conform as quietly as we can to the
vulgar notions which are connected with this, and take up
the theology of the vulgar as well as their politics.   But
if we think this necessity rather imaginary than real, we
should renounce their dreams of society, together with
their visions of religion, and vindicate ourselves into perfect liberty."

The most interesting fact about this spirited performance is, that it is a satirical literary handling of the great

proposition which Burke enforced, with all the thunder and lurid effulgence of his most passionate rhetoric, five-and-thirty years later. This proposition is that the world would fall into ruin, "if the practice of all moral duties, and the foundations of society, rested upon having their reasons made clear and demonstrative to every individual." The satire is intended for an illustration of what with Burke was the cardinal truth for men, namely, that if you encourage every individual to let the imagination loose upon all subjects, without any restraint from a sense of his own weakness, and his subordinate rank in the long scheme of things, then there is nothing of all that the opinion of ages has agreed to regard as excellent and venerable, which would not be exposed to destruction at the hands of rationalistic criticism. This was Burke's most fundamental and unswerving conviction from the first piece that he wrote down to the last, and down to the last hour of his existence.

It is a coincidence worth noticing that only two years before the appearance of the *Vindication*, Rousseau had published the second of the two memorable Discourses in which he insisted with serious eloquence on that which Burke treats as a triumph of irony. He believed, and many thousands of Frenchmen came to a speculative agreement with him, that artificial society had marked a decline in the felicity of man, and there are passages in the Discourse in which he demonstrates this, that are easily interchangeable with passages in the *Vindication*. Who would undertake to tell us from internal evidence whether the following page, with its sombre glow, is an extract from Burke, or an extract from the book which Rousseau begins by the sentence that man is born free, yet is he everywhere in chains?

There are in Great Britain upwards of a hundred thousand people employed in lead, tin, iron, copper, and coal mines; these unhappy wretches scarce ever see the light of the sun; they are buried in the bowels of the earth; there they work at a severe and dismal task, without the least prospect of being delivered from it; they subsist upon the coarsest and worst sort of fare; they have their health miserably impaired, and their lives cut short, by being perpetually confined in the close vapour of these malignant minerals. A hundred thousand more at least are tortured without remission by the suffocating smoke, intense fires, and constant drudgery, necessary in refining and managing the products of those mines. If any man informed us that two hundred thousand innocent persons were condemned to so intolerable slavery, how should we pity the unhappy sufferers, and how great would be our just indignation against those who inflicted so cruel and ignominious a punishment! . . . But this number, considerable as it is, and the slavery, with all its baseness and horror, which we have at home, is nothing to what the rest of the world affords of the same nature. Millions daily bathed in the poisonous damps and destructive effluvia of lead, silver, copper, and arsenic, to say nothing of those other employments, those stations of wretchedness and contempt, in which civil society has placed the numerous *enfans perdus* of her army. Would any rational man submit to one of the most tolerable of these drudgeries, for all the artificial enjoyments which policy has made to result from them? . . . Indeed, the blindness of one part of mankind co-operating with the frenzy and villany of the other, has been the real builder of this respectable fabric of political society: and as the blindness of mankind has caused their slavery, in return their state of slavery is made a pretence for continuing them in a state of blindness; for the politician will tell you gravely, that their life of servitude disqualifies the greater part of the race of man for a search of truth, and supplies them with no other than mean and insufficient ideas. This is but too true; and this is one of the reasons for which I blame such institutions.

From the very beginning, therefore, Burke was drawn to the deepest of all the currents in the thought of the eighteenth century. Johnson and Goldsmith continued

the traditions of social and polite literature which had been
established by the Queen Anne men. Warburton and a
whole host of apologists carried on the battle against deism and infidelity. Hume, after furnishing the arsenal of
scepticism with a new array of deadlier engines and more
abundant ammunition, had betaken himself placidly to the
composition of history. What is remarkable in Burke's
first performance is his discernment of the important fact,
that behind the intellectual disturbances in the sphere of
philosophy, and the noisier agitations in the sphere of theology, there silently stalked a force that might shake the
whole fabric of civil society itself. In France, as all students of its speculative history are agreed, there came a
time in the eighteenth century when theological controversy was turned into political controversy. Innovators
left the question about the truth of Christianity, and busied themselves with questions about the ends and means
of governments. The appearance of Burke's *Vindication
of Natural Society* coincides in time with the beginning
of this important transformation. Burke foresaw from
the first what, if rationalism were allowed to run an unim-
peded course, would be the really great business of the second half of his century.

If in his first book Burke showed how alive he was to
the profound movement of the time, in the second he dealt
with one of the most serious of its more superficial interests. The essay on the Sublime and Beautiful fell in with
a set of topics, on which the curiosity of the better minds
of the age, alike in France, England, and Germany, was
fully stirred. In England the essay has been ordinarily
slighted; it has perhaps been overshadowed by its author's
fame in weightier matters. The nearest approach to a full
and serious treatment of its main positions is to be found

2

in Dugald Stewart's lectures. The great rhetorical art-critic of our own day refers to it in words of disparagement, and in truth it has none of the flummery of modern criticism. It is a piece of hard thinking, and it has the distinction of having interested and stimulated Lessing, the author of *Laoköon* (1766), by far the most definitely valuable of all the contributions to æsthetic thought in an age which was not poor in them. Lessing was so struck with the *Inquiry* that he set about a translation of it, and the correspondence between him and Moses Mendelssohn on the questions which Burke had raised, contains the germs of the doctrine as to poetry and painting which *Laoköon* afterwards made so famous. Its influence on Lessing and on Kant was such as to justify the German historian of the literature of the century in bestowing on it the coveted epithet of epoch-making.

The book is full of crudities. We feel the worse side of the eighteenth century when Burke tells us that a thirst for Variety in architecture is sure to leave very little true taste; or that an air of robustness and strength is very prejudicial to beauty; or that sad fuscous colours are indispensable for sublimity. Many of the sections, again, are little more than expanded definitions from the dictionary. Any tiro may now be shocked at such a proposition as that beauty acts by relaxing the solids of the whole system. But at least one signal merit remains to the *Inquiry*. It was a vigorous enlargement of the principle, which Addison had not long before timidly illustrated, that critics of art seek its principles in the wrong place, so long as they limit their search to poems, pictures, engravings, statues, and buildings, instead of first arranging the sentiments and faculties in man to which art makes its appeal. Addison's treatment was slight, and merely literary; Burke dealt boldly with his subject on the base of the most scientific psychology that was then within his reach. To approach it on the psychological side at all, was to make a distinct and remarkable advance in the method of the inquiry which he had taken in hand.

CHAPTER II.

BURKE was thirty years old before he approached even the threshold of the arena in which he was destined to be so great a figure. He had made a mark in literature, and it was to literature rather than to public affairs that his ambition turned. He had naturally become acquainted with the brother authors who haunted the coffee-houses in Fleet Street; and Burke, along with his father-in-law, Dr. Nugent, was one of the first members of the immortal club where Johnson did conversational battle with all comers. We shall, in a later chapter, have something to say on Burke's friendships with the followers of his first profession, and on the active sympathy with which he helped those who were struggling into authorship. Meanwhile, the fragments that remain of his own attempts in this direction are no considerable contributions. His *Hints for an Essay on the Drama* are jejune and infertile, when compared with the vigorous and original thought of Diderot and Lessing at about the same period. He wrote an Account of the European Settlements in America. His *Abridgment of the History of England* comes down no further than to the reign of John. A much more important undertaking than his history of the past, was his design for a yearly chronicle of the present. The *Annual Register* began to appear in 1759. Dodsley, the bookseller of Pall Mall, provided the sinews of war, and he gave Burke a hundred pounds a year for his survey of the great events which were then passing in the world. The scheme was probably born of the circumstances of the hour, for this was the climax of the Seven Years' War. The clang of arms was heard in every quarter of the globe, and in East and West new lands were being brought under the dominion of Great Britain.

In this exciting crisis of national affairs, Burke began to be acquainted with public men. In 1759 he was introduced, probably by Lord Charlemont, to William Gerard Hamilton, who only survives in our memories by his nickname of Single-speech. As a matter of fact, he made many speeches in Parliament, and some good ones, but none so good as the first, delivered in a debate in 1755, in which Pitt, Fox, Grenville, and Murray all took part, and were all outshone by the new luminary. But the new luminary never shone again with its first brilliance. He sought Burke out on the strength of the success of the *Vindication of Natural Society*, and he seems to have had a taste for good company. Horace Walpole describes a dinner at his house in the summer of 1761. " There were Garrick," he says, " and a young Mr. Burke, who wrote a book in the style of Lord Bolingbroke, that is much admired. He is a sensible man, but has not worn off his authorism yet, and thinks there is nothing so charming as writers, and to be one. He will know better one of these days." The prophecy came true in time, but it was Burke's passion for authorism that eventually led to a rupture with his first patron. Hamilton was a man of ability, but selfish and unreasonable. Dr. Leland afterwards described him compendiously as a sullen, vain, proud, selfish, canker-hearted, envious reptile.

In 1761 Hamilton went to Ireland as secretary to Lord Halifax, and Burke accompanied him in some indefinite capacity. "The absenteeism of her men of genius," an eminent historian has said, "was a worse wrong to Ireland than the absenteeism of her landlords. If Edmund Burke had remained in the country where Providence had placed him, he might have changed the current of its history."[1] It is at least to be said that Burke was never so absorbed in other affairs, as to forget the peculiar interests of his native land. We have his own word, and his career does not belie it, that in the elation with which he was filled on being elected a member of Parliament, what was first and uppermost in his thoughts was the hope of being somewhat useful to the place of his birth and education; and to the last he had in it "a dearness of instinct more than he could justify to reason." In fact the affairs of Ireland had a most important part in Burke's life at one or two critical moments, and this is as convenient a place as we are likely to find for describing in a few words what were the issues. The brief space can hardly be grudged in an account of a great political writer, for Ireland has furnished the chief ordeal, test, and standard of English statesmen.

Ireland in the middle of the eighteenth century was to England just what the American colonies would have been, if they had contained, besides the European settlers, more than twice their number of unenslaved negroes. After the suppression of the great rebellion of Tyrconnel by William of Orange, nearly the whole of the land was confiscated, the peasants were made beggars and outlaws, the Penal Laws against the Catholics were enacted and enforced, and the grand reign of Protestant Ascendancy began in all its

[1] Froude's *Ireland,* ii. 214.

vileness and completeness. The Protestants and landlords
were supreme; the peasants and the Catholics were prostrate in despair. The Revolution brought about in Ireland
just the reverse of what it effected in England. Here it
delivered the body of the nation from the attempted
supremacy of a small sect. There it made a small sect
supreme over the body of the nation. "It was, to say the
truth," Burke wrote, "not a revolution but a conquest,"
and the policy of conquest was treated as the just and
normal system of government. The last conquest of England was in the eleventh century. The last conquest of
Ireland was at the very end of the seventeenth.

Sixty years after these events, when Burke revisited Ireland, some important changes had taken place. The English settlers of the beginning of the century had formed
an Irish interest. They had become Anglo-Irish, just as
the colonists still further west had formed a colonial interest and become Anglo-American. The same conduct on the
part of the mother country promoted the growth of these
hostile interests in both cases. The commercial policy
pursued by England towards America was identical with
that pursued towards Ireland. The industry of the Anglo-
Irish traders was restricted, their commerce and even their
production fettered, their prosperity checked, for the benefit of the merchants of Manchester and Bristol. *Crescit
Roma Albæ ruinis.* "The bulk of the people," said Stone,
the Primate, "are not regularly either lodged, clothed, or
fed; and those things which in England are called necessaries of life, are to us only accidents, and we can, and in
many places do, subsist without them." On the other
hand, the peasantry had gradually taken heart to resent
their spoliation and attempted extirpation, and in 1761
their misery under the exactions of landlords and a church

which tried to spread Christianity by the brotherly agency
of the tithe-proctor, gave birth to Whiteboyism—a terrible
spectre, which, under various names and with various modifications, has ridden Ireland down to our own time.

Burke saw the Protestant traders of the dependency the
victims of the colonial and commercial system; the Catholic land-owners legally dispossessed by the operation of the
penal laws; the Catholic peasantry deeply penetrated with
an insurgent and vindictive spirit; and the imperial government standing very much aloof, and leaving the country to the tender mercies of the Undertakers and some
Protestant churchmen. The Anglo-Irish were bitterly dis-
contented with the mother country; and the Catholic native Irish were regarded by their Protestant oppressors
with exactly that combination of intense contempt and
loathing, and intense rage and terror, which their American
counterpart would have divided between the Negro and
the Red Indian. To the Anglo-Irish the native peasant
was as odious as the first, and as terrible as the second.
Even at the close of the century Burke could declare that
the various descriptions of the people were kept as much
apart, as if they were not only separate nations, but separate species. There were thousands, he says, who had
never talked to a Roman Catholic in their whole lives, unless they happened to talk to a gardener's workman, or
some other labourer of the second or third order, while a
little time before this they were so averse to have them
near their persons, that they would not employ even those
who could never find their way beyond the stables. Chesterfield, a thoroughly impartial and just observer, said in
1764 that the poor people in Ireland were used worse than
negroes by their masters and the middlemen. We should
never forget that in the transactions with the English gov-

ernment during the eighteenth century, the people concerned were not the Irish, but the Anglo-Irish, the colonists
of 1691. They were an aristocracy, as Adam Smith said
of them, not founded in the natural and respectable distinctions of birth and fortune, but in the most odious of
all distinctions, those of religious and political prejudices
—distinctions which, more than any other, animate both
the insolence of the oppressors, and the hatred and indignation of the oppressed.

The directions in which Irish improvement would move,
were clear from the middle of the century to men with
much less foresight than Burke had. The removal of all
commercial restrictions, either by Independence or Union,
on the one hand; and the gradual emancipation of the
Catholics, on the other; were the two processes to which
every consideration of good government manifestly pointed. The first proved a much shorter and simpler process
than the second. To the first the only obstacle was the
blindness and selfishness of the English merchants. The
second had to overcome the virulent opposition of the ty-
rannical Protestant faction in Ireland, and the disgrace-
ful but deep-rooted antipathies of the English nation.
The history of the relation between the mother country
and her dependency during Burke's life, may be charac-
terized as a commercial and legislative struggle between
the imperial government and the Anglo-Irish interest, in
which each side for its own convenience, as the turn served,
drew support from the Catholic majority.

A Whiteboy outbreak, attended by the usual circumstances of disorder and violence, took place while Burke
was in Ireland. It suited the interests of faction to represent these commotions as the symptoms of a deliberate
rebellion. The malcontents were represented as carrying
2*

on treasonable correspondence, sometimes with Spain and
sometimes with France; they were accused of receiving
money and arms from their foreign sympathizers, and of
aiming at throwing off the English rule. Burke says that
he had means and the desire of informing himself to the
bottom upon the matter, and he came strongly to the conclusion that this was not a true view of what had happened. What had happened was due, he thought, to no plot,
but to superficial and fortuitous circumstances. He con-
sequently did not shrink from describing it as criminal,
that the king's Catholic subjects in Ireland should have
been subjected, on no good grounds, to harassing persecution, and that numbers of them should have been ruined
in fortune, imprisoned, tried, and capitally executed for a
rebellion which was no rebellion at all. The episode is
only important as illustrating the strong and manly temper in which Burke, unlike too many of his countrymen
with fortunes to make by English favour, uniformly considered the circumstances of his country. It was not until a later time that he had an opportunity of acting con-
spicuously on her behalf, but whatever influence he came
to acquire with his party was unflinchingly used against
the cruelty of English prejudice.

Burke appears to have remained in Ireland for two years
(1761–3). In 1763 Hamilton, who had found him an
invaluable auxiliary, procured for him, principally with
the aid of the Primate Stone, a pension of three hundred
pounds a year from the Irish Treasury. In thanking him
for this service, Burke proceeded to bargain that the obligation should not bind him to give to his patron the whole
of his time. He insisted on being left with a discreet liberty to continue a little work which he had as a rent-
charge upon his thoughts. Whatever advantages he had

acquired, he says, had been due to literary reputation, and he could only hope for a continuance of such advantages on condition of doing something to keep the same reputation alive. What this literary design was we do not know with certainty. It is believed to have been a history of England, of which, as I have said, a fragment remains. Whatever the work may have been, it was an offence to Hamilton. With an irrational stubbornness that may well astound us when we think of the noble genius that he thus wished to confine to paltry personal duties, he persisted that Burke should bind himself to his service for life, and to the exclusion of other interests. "To circumscribe my hopes," cried Burke, "to give up even the possibility of liberty, to annihilate myself for ever!" He threw up the pension, which he had held for two years, and declined all further connexion with Hamilton, whom he roundly described as an infamous scoundrel. "Six of the best years of my life he took me from every pursuit of my literary reputation, or of improvement of my fortune. . . . In all this time you may easily conceive how much I felt at seeing myself left behind by almost all of my contemporaries. There never was a season more favourable for any man who chose to enter into the career of public life; and I think I am not guilty of ostentation in supposing my own moral character, and my industry, my friends and connexions, when Mr. Hamilton first sought my acquaintance, were not at all inferior to those of several whose fortune is at this day upon a very different footing from mine."

It was not long before a more important opening offered itself, which speedily brought Burke into the main stream of public life. In the summer of 1765 a change of ministry took place. It was the third since the king's accession five years ago. First, Pitt had been disgraced, and

the old Duke of Newcastle dismissed. Then Bute came
into power, but Bute quailed before the storm of calumny
and hate which his Scotch nationality, and the supposed
source of his power over the king, had raised in every
town in England.   After Lord Bute, George Grenville
undertook the Government.   Before he had been many
months in office, he had sown the seeds of war in the colonies, wearied parliament, and disgusted the king.   In
June, 1765, Grenville was dismissed.   With profound reluctance the king had no other choice than to summon
Lord Rockingham, and Lord Rockingham, in a happy moment for himself and his party, was induced to offer Burke
a post as his private secretary.   A government by country
gentlemen is too apt to be a government of ignorance,
and Lord Rockingham was without either experience or
knowledge.   He felt, or friends felt for him, the advantage
of having at his side a man who was chiefly known as an
author in the service of Dodsley, and as having conducted
the *Annual Register* with great ability, but who even then
was widely spoken of as nothing less than an encyclopædia
of political knowledge.

It is commonly believed that Burke was commended to
Lord Rockingham by William Fitzherbert.   Fitzherbert
was President of the Board of Trade in the new government, but he is more likely to be remembered as Dr. Johnson's famous example of the truth of the observation, that
a man will please more upon the whole by negative qualities than by positive, because he was the most acceptable
man in London, and yet overpowered nobody by the superiority of his talents, made no man think worse of himself
by being his rival, seemed always to listen, did not oblige
you to hear much from him, and did not oppose what
you said.   Besides Fitzherbert's influence, we have it on

Burke's own authority that his promotion was partly due
to that mysterious person, William Burke, who was at the
same time appointed an under-secretary of state.   There
must have been unpleasant rumours afloat as to the Burke
connexion, and we shall presently consider what they were
worth.   Meanwhile, it is enough to say that the old Duke
of Newcastle hurried to the new premier, and told him
the appointment would never do : that the new secretary
was not only an Irish adventurer, which was true, but that
he was an Irish papist, which was not true ; that he was
a Jesuit, that he was a spy from Saint Omer's, and that
his real name was O'Bourke.   Lord Rockingham behaved
like a man of sense and honour, sent for Burke, and repeated to him what he had heard.   Burke warmly denounced the truthlessness of the Duke's tattle : he insisted
that the reports which his chief had heard would probably, even unknown to himself, create in his mind such
suspicions as would stand in the way of a thorough confidence.   No earthly consideration, he said, should induce
him to continue in relations with a man whose trust in
him was not entire ; and he pressed his resignation.   To
this Lord Rockingham would not consent, and from that
time until his death, seventeen years afterwards, the relations between them were those of loyal and honourable
service on the one hand, and generous and appreciative
friendship on the other.   Six-and-twenty years afterwards
(1791) Burke remembered the month in which he had
first become connected with a man whose memory, he said,
will ever be precious to Englishmen of all parties, as long
as the ideas of honour and virtue, public and private, are
understood and cherished in this nation.

The Rockingham ministry remained in office for a year
and twenty days (1765–6).   About the middle of this

term (Dec. 26, 1765), Burke was returned to Parliament
for the borough of Wendover, by the influence of Lord
Verney, who owned it, and who also returned William
Burke for another borough. Lord Verney was an Irish
peer, with large property in Buckinghamshire; he now
represented that county in Parliament. It was William
Burke's influence with Lord Verney that procured for his
namesake the seat at Wendover. Burke made his first
speech in the House of Commons a few days after the
opening of the session of 1766 (Jan. 27), and was honoured by a compliment from Pitt, still the Great Commoner.
A week later he spoke again on the same momentous
theme, the complaints of the American colonists, and his
success was so marked that good judges predicted, in the
stiff phraseology of the time, that he would soon add the
palm of the orator to the laurel of the writer and the philosopher. The friendly Dr. Johnson wrote to Langton,
that Burke had gained more reputation than any man at
his first appearance had ever gained before. The session
was a great triumph to the new member, but it brought
neither strength nor popularity to the administration. At
the end of it, the king dismissed them, and the Chatham
government was formed; that strange combination which
has been made famous by Burke's description of it, as a
piece of joinery so crossly indented and whimsically dove-
tailed, such a piece of diversified mosaic, such a tesselated
pavement without cement, that it was indeed a very curious show, but utterly unsafe to touch and unsure to stand
upon. There was no obvious reason why Burke should
not have joined the new ministry. The change was at
first one of persons, rather than of principles or of measures. To put himself, as Burke afterwards said, out of
the way of the negotiations which were then being carried

on very eagerly and through many channels with the Earl
of Chatham, he went to Ireland very soon after the change
of ministry. He was free from party engagements, and
more than this, he was free at the express desire of his
friends; for on the very day of his return, the Marquis of
Rockingham wished him to accept office under the new
system. Burke "believes he might have had such a situation, but he cheerfully took his fate with his party." In
a short time he rendered his party the first of a long series
of splendid literary services by writing his *Observations on
the Present State of the Nation* (1769). It was a reply
to a pamphlet by George Grenville, in which the disappointed minister accused his successors of ruining the country. Burke, in answering the charge, showed a grasp of
commercial and fiscal details at least equal to that of Grenville himself, then considered the first man of his time in
dealing with the national trade and resources. To this
easy mastery of the special facts of the discussion, Burke
added the far rarer art of lighting them up by broad principles, and placing himself and his readers at the highest
and most effective point of view for commanding their
general bearings.

If Burke had been the Irish adventurer that his enemies
described, he might well have seized with impatience the
opening to office that the recent exhibition of his powers
in the House of Commons had now made accessible to
him. There was not a man in Great Britain to whom the
emoluments of office would have been more useful. It is
one of the standing mysteries in literary biography, how
Burke could think of entering Parliament without any
means that anybody can now trace of earning a fitting
livelihood. Yet at this time Burke, whom we saw not
long ago writing for the booksellers, had become affluent

enough to pay a yearly allowance to Barry, the painter,
in order to enable him to study the pictures in the great
European galleries, and to make a prolonged residence at
Rome. A little later he took a step which makes the riddle still more difficult, and which has given abundant employment to wits who are *maximi in minimis*, and think
that every question which they can ask, yet to which history has thought it worth while to leave no answer, is
somehow a triumph of their own learning and dialectic.

In 1769 Burke purchased a house and lands known as
Gregories, in the parishes of Penn and Beaconsfield, in the
county of Bucks. It has often been asked, and naturally
enough, how a man who, hardly more than a few months
before, was still contented to earn an extra hundred pounds
a year by writing for Dodsley, should now have launched
out as the buyer of a fine house and estate, which cost upwards of twenty-two thousand pounds, which could not be
kept up on less than two thousand five hundred a year,
and of which the returns did not amount to one-fifth of
that sum.   Whence did he procure the money, and what
is perhaps more difficult to answer, how came he first to
entertain the idea of a design so ill-proportioned to anything that we can now discern in his means and prospects?
The common answer from Burke's enemies, and even from
some neutral inquirers, gives to every lover of this great
man's high character an unpleasant shock.   It is alleged
that he had plunged into furious gambling in East India
stock.   The charge was current at the time, and it was
speedily revived when Burke's abandonment of his party,
after the French Revolution, exposed him to a thousand
attacks of reckless and uncontrolled virulence.   It has been
stirred by one or two pertinacious critics nearer our own
time, and none of the biographers have dealt with the per-

plexities of the matter as they ought to have done.   Nobody, indeed, has ever pretended to find one jot or tittle of direct evidence that Burke himself took a part in the gambling in India or other stocks.   There is evidence that he was a holder of the stock, and no more.   But what is undeniable is that Richard Burke, his brother, William Burke, his intimate if not his kinsman, and Lord Verney, his political patron, were all three at this time engaged together in immense transactions in East India stock; that in 1769 the stock fell violently; that they were unable to pay their differences; and that in the very year in which Edmund Burke bought Gregories, they were utterly ruined, two of them beyond retrieval.   Again it is clear that, after this, Richard Burke was engaged in land-jobbing in the West Indies; that his claims were disputed by the Government as questionable and dishonest; and that he lost his case. Edmund Burke was said, in the gossip of the day, to be deeply interested in land at Saint Vincent's.   But there is no evidence.   What cannot be denied is that an unpleasant taint of speculation and financial adventurership hung at one time about the whole connexion, and that the adventures invariably came to an unlucky end.

Whether Edmund Burke and William Burke were relations or not, and if so, in what degree they were relations, neither of them ever knew; they believed that their fathers sometimes called one another cousins, and that was all that they had to say on the subject.   But they were as intimate as brothers, and when William Burke went to mend his broken fortunes in India, Edmund Burke commended him to Philip Francis—then fighting his deadly duel of five years with Warren Hastings at Calcutta—as one whom he had tenderly loved, highly valued, and continually lived with in an union not to be expressed, quite

since their boyish years. "Looking back to the course of
my life," he wrote in 1771, "I remember no one considerable benefit in the whole of it which I did not, mediately or immediately, derive from William Burke." There is
nothing intrinsically incredible, therefore, considering this
intimacy and the community of purse and home which
subsisted among the three Burkes, in the theory that when
Edmund Burke bought his property in Buckinghamshire,
he looked for help from the speculations of Richard and
William. However this may have been, from them no
help came. Many years afterwards (1783), Lord Verney
filed a bill in Chancery claiming from Edmund Burke a
sum of 6000*l*., which he alleged that he had lent at the
instigation of William Burke to assist in completing the
purchase of Beaconsfield. Burke's sworn answer denied
all knowledge of the transaction, and the plaintiff did not
get the relief for which he had prayed.

In a letter to Shackleton (May 1, 1768) Burke gave the
following account of what he had done:—"I have made
a push," he says, "with all I could collect of my own, and
the aid of my friends, to cast a little root in this country.
I have purchased a house, with an estate of about six hundred acres of land, in Buckinghamshire, twenty-four miles
from London. It is a place exceedingly pleasant; and I
propose, God willing, to become a farmer in good earnest.
You who are classical will not be displeased to know that
it was formerly the seat of Waller, the poet, whose house,
or part of it, makes at present the farm-house within an
hundred yards of me." The details of the actual purchase
of Beaconsfield have been made tolerably clear. The price
was twenty-two thousand pounds, more or less. Fourteen
thousand were left on mortgage, which remained outstand-
ing until the sale of the property by Mrs. Burke in 1812.

Garret Burke, the elder brother, had shortly before the purchase made Edmund his residuary legatee, and this bequest is rather conjecturally estimated at two thousand pounds. The balance of six thousand was advanced by Lord Rockingham on Burke's bond.

The purchase after all was the smallest part of the matter, and it still remains a puzzle not only how Burke was able to maintain so handsome an establishment, but how he could ever suppose it likely that he would be able to maintain it. He counted, no doubt, on making some sort of income by farming, but then he might well have known that an absorbed politician would hardly be able, as he called it, to turn farmer in good earnest. For a short time he received a salary of seven hundred pounds a year as agent for New York. We may perhaps take for granted that he made as much more out of his acres. He received something from Dodsley for his work on the *Annual Register* down to 1788. But when all these resources have been counted up, we cannot but see the gulf of a great yearly deficit. The unhappy truth is that from the middle of 1769, when we find him applying to Garrick for the loan of a thousand pounds, down to 1794, when the king gave him a pension, Burke was never free from the harassing strain of debts and want of money. It has been stated with good show of authority, that his obligations to Lord Rockingham amounted to not less than thirty thousand pounds. When that nobleman died (1782), with a generosity which is not the less honourable to him for having been so richly earned by the faithful friend who was the object of it, he left instructions to his executors that all Burke's bonds should be destroyed.

We may indeed wish from the bottom of our hearts that all this had been otherwise. But those who press it

as a reproach against Burke's memory may be justly reminded that when Pitt died, after drawing the pay of a
minister for twenty years, he left debts to the amount of
forty thousand pounds. Burke, as I have said elsewhere,
had none of the vices of profusion, but he had that quality
which Aristotle places high among the virtues—the noble
mean of Magnificence, standing midway between the two
extremes of vulgar ostentation and narrow pettiness.   At
least, every creditor was paid in good time, and nobody
suffered but himself. Those who think these disagreeable
matters of supreme importance, and allow such things to
stand between them and Burke's greatness, are like the
people—slightly to alter a figure from a philosopher of
old—who, when they went to Olympia, could only perceive that they were scorched by the sun, and pressed by
the crowd, and deprived of comfortable means of bathing,
and wetted by the rain, and that life was full of disagreeable and troublesome things, and so they almost forgot the
great colossus of ivory and gold, Phidias's statue of Zeus,
which they had come to see, and which stood in all its
glory and power before their perturbed and foolish vision.

There have been few men in history with whom personal objects counted for so little as they counted with
Burke.   He really did what so many public men only
feign to do.   He forgot that he had any interests of his
own to be promoted, apart from the interests of the party
with which he acted, and from those of the whole nation,
for which he held himself a trustee.   What William
Burke said of him in 1766 was true throughout his life
—" Ned is full of real business, intent upon doing solid
good to his country, as much as if he was to receive twenty
per cent. from the Empire."   Such men as the shrewd and
impudent Rigby atoned for a plebeian origin by the arts

of dependence and a judicious servility, and drew more
of the public money from the pay office in half-a-dozen
quarter-days than Burke received in all his life. It was
not by such arts that Burke rose. When we remember
all the untold bitterness of the struggle in which he was
engaged, from the time when the old Duke of Newcastle
tried to make the Marquis of Rockingham dismiss his new
private secretary as an Irish Jesuit in disguise (1765),
down to the time when the Duke of Bedford, himself bat-
tening "in grants to the house of Russell, so enormous as
not only to outrage economy, but even to stagger credibil-
ity," assailed the government for giving Burke a moderate
pension, we may almost imagine that if Johnson had imitated the famous Tenth Satire a little later, he would have
been tempted to apply the poet's cynical criticism of the
career heroic to the greater Cicero of his own day. "I
was not," Burke said, in a passage of lofty dignity, "like
his Grace of Bedford, swaddled and rocked and dandled
into a legislator; *Nitor in adversum* is the motto for a
man like me. I possessed not one of the qualities, nor
cultivated one of the arts, that recommend men to the favour and protection of the great. I was not made for a
minion or a tool. As little did I follow the trade of winning the hearts, by imposing on the understandings of the
people. At every step of my progress in life, for in every
step was I traversed and opposed, and at every turnpike I
met I was obliged to show my passport, and again and
again to prove my sole title to the honour of being useful
to my country, by a proof that I was not wholly unac-
quainted with its laws, and the whole system of its interests both abroad and at home; otherwise no rank, no toleration even for me."

CHAPTER III.

THE CONSTITUTIONAL STRUGGLE.

FOREIGN observers of our affairs looked upon the state of England between the accession of George III. and the loss of the American colonies (1760–1776), with mixed disgust and satisfaction. Their instinct as absolute rulers was revolted by a spectacle of unbridled faction and raging anarchy; their envy was soothed by the growing weakness of a power which Chatham had so short a time before left at the highest point of grandeur and strength. Frederick the Great spoke with contempt of the insolence of Opposition and the virulence of parties; and vowed that, petty German prince as he was, he would not change places with the King of England. The Emperor Joseph pronounced positively that Great Britain was declining, that Parliament was ruining itself, and that the colonies threatened a catastrophe. Catherine of Russia thought that nothing would restore its ancient vigour to the realm, short of the bracing and heroic remedy of a war. Even at home, such shrewd and experienced onlookers as Horace Walpole suspected that the state of the country was more serious than it had been since the Great Rebellion, and declared it to be approaching by fast strides to some sharp crisis. Men who remembered their Roman history, fancied that they saw every symptom of confusion that preceded the ruin of the Commonwealth, and began to inquire uneasily what was the temper of the army. Men who remembered the story of the violence and insatiable factiousness of Florence, turned again to Macchiavelli and to Guicciardini, to trace a parallel between the fierce city on the Arno and the fierce city on the Thames. When the King of Sweden, in 1772, carried out a revolution, by abolishing an oligarchic council and assuming the powers of a dictator, with the assent of his people, there were actually serious men in England who thought that the English, after having been guilty of every meanness and corruption, would soon, like the Swedes, own themselves unworthy to be free. The Duke of Richmond, who happened to have a claim to a peerage and an estate in France, excused himself for taking so much pains to establish his claim to them, by gravely asking who knew that a time might not soon come when England would not be worthy living in, and when a retreat to France might be a very happy thing for a free man to have?

The reign had begun by a furious outbreak of hatred between the English and the Scotch. Lord Bute had been driven from office, not merely because he was supposed to owe his power to a scandalous friendship with the King's mother, but because he was accused of crowding the public service with his detested countrymen from the other side of the Tweed. He fell, less from disapproval of his policy than from rude prejudice against his country. The flow of angry emotion had not subsided before the whisper of strife in the American colonies began to trouble the air; and before that had waxed loud, the Middlesex election had blown into a portentous hurricane. This was the first great constitutional case after Burke came into the House of Commons. As, moreover, it became a leading element in the crisis which was the occasion of

Burke's first remarkable essay in the literature of politics, it is as well to go over the facts.

The Parliament to which he had first been returned, now approaching the expiry of its legal term, was dissolved in the spring of 1768. Wilkes, then an outlaw in Paris, returned to England, and announced himself as a candidate for the City. When the election was over, his name stood last on the poll. But his ancient fame as the opponent and victim of the court five years before were revived. After his rejection in the City, he found himself strong enough to stand for the county of Middlesex. Here he was returned at the head of the poll after an excited election. Wilkes had been tried in 1764, and found guilty by the King's Bench of republishing Number Forty-five of the *North Briton*, and of printing and publishing the *Essay on Woman*. He had not appeared to receive sentence, and had been outlawed in consequence. After his election for Middlesex, he obtained a reversal of his outlawry on the point of technical form. He then came up for sentence under the original verdict. The court sent him to prison for twenty-two months, and condemned him to pay a fine of a thousand pounds.

Wilkes was in prison when the second session of the new Parliament began. His case came before the House in November, 1768, on his own petition, accusing Lord Mansfield of altering the record at his trial. After many acrimonious debates and examinations of Wilkes and others at the bar of the House, at length, by 219 votes against 136, the famous motion was passed which expelled him from the House. Another election for Middlesex was now held, and Wilkes was returned without opposition. The day after the return, the House of Commons resolved, by an immense majority, that, having been expelled, Wilkes

was incapable of serving in that Parliament. The following month Wilkes was once more elected. The House
once more declared the election void. In April another
election took place, and this time the Government put forward Colonel Luttrell, who vacated his seat for Bossiney
for the purpose of opposing Wilkes. There was the same
result, and for the fourth time Wilkes was at the head of
the poll. The House ordered the return to be altered,
and after hearing by counsel the freeholders of Middlesex
who petitioned against the alteration, finally confirmed it
(May 8, 1769) by a majority of 221 to 152. According
to Lord Temple, this was the greatest majority ever known
on the last day of a session.

The purport and significance of these arbitrary proceedings need little interpretation. The House, according to
the authorities, had a constitutional right to expel Wilkes,
though the grounds on which even this is defended would
probably be questioned if a similar case were to arise in
our own day. But a single branch of the legislature could
have no power to pass an incapacitating vote either against
Wilkes or anybody else. An Act of Parliament is the
least instrument by which such incapacity could be imposed. The House might perhaps expel Wilkes, but it
could not either legally, or with regard to the less definite
limits of constitutional morality, decide whom the Middlesex freeholders should not elect, and it could not therefore
set aside their representative, who was then free from any
disabling quality. Lord Camden did not much exagger-
ate, when he declared in a debate on the subject in the
House of Lords, that the judgment passed upon the Middlesex election had given the constitution a more dangerous wound than any which were given during the twelve
years' absence of Parliament in the reign of Charles I.

3

The House of Commons was usurping another form of
that very dispensing power, for pretending to which the
last of the Stuart sovereigns had lost his crown. If the
House by a vote could deprive Wilkes of a right to sit,
what legal or constitutional impediment would there be in
the way, if the majority were at any time disposed to declare all their most formidable opponents in the minority
incapable of sitting?

In the same Parliament, there was another and scarcely
less remarkable case of Privilege, "that eldest son of Prerogative," as Burke truly called it, "and inheriting all the
vices of its parent." Certain printers were accused of
breach of privilege for reporting the debates of the House
(March, 1771). The messenger of the serjeant-at-arms
attempted to take one of them into custody in his own
shop in the City. A constable was standing by, designed-
ly, it has been supposed, and Miller, the printer, gave the
messenger into his custody for an assault. The case came
on before the Lord Mayor, Alderman Wilkes, and Alderman Oliver, the same evening, and the result was that the
messenger of the House was committed. The City doctrine was, that if the House of Commons had a serjeant-
at-arms, they had a serjeant-at-mace. If the House of
Commons could send their citizens to Newgate, they could
send its messenger to the Compter. Two other printers
were collusively arrested, brought before Wilkes and Oliver, and at once liberated.

The Commons instantly resolved on stern measures.
The Lord Mayor and Oliver were taken and dispatched to
the Tower, where they lay until the prorogation of Parliament. Wilkes stubbornly refused to pay any attention to
repeated summonses to attend at the bar of the House,
very properly insisting that he ought to be summoned to

attend *in his place* as member for Middlesex. Besides committing Crosby and Oliver to the Tower, the House summoned the Lord Mayor's clerk to attend with his books, and then and there forced him to strike out the record of the recognisances into which their messenger had entered on being committed at the Mansion House. No Stuart ever did anything more arbitrary and illegal. The House deliberately intended to constitute itself, as Burke had said two years before, an arbitrary and despotic assembly. "The distempers of monarchy were the great subjects of apprehension and redress in the last century. In this, the distempers of Parliament."

Burke, in a speech which he delivered in his place in 1771, warned the House of the evils of the course upon which they were entering, and declared those to be their mortal enemies who would persuade them to act as if they were a self-originated magistracy, independent of the people, and unconnected with their opinions and feelings. But these mortal enemies of its very constitution were at this time the majority of the House. It was to no purpose that Burke argued with more than legal closeness that incapacitation could not be a power according to law, inasmuch as it had neither of the two properties of law: it was not *known*, "you yourself not knowing upon what grounds you will vote the incapacity of any man ;" and it was not *fixed*, because it was varied according to the occasion, exercised according to discretion, and no man could call for it as a right. A strain of unanswerable reasoning of this kind counted for nothing, in spite of its being unanswerable. Despotic or oligarchic pretensions are proof against the most formidable battery that reason and experience can construct against them. And Wilkes's exclusion endured until this Parliament—the Unreported Parlia-

ment, as it was called, and in many respects the very worst
that ever assembled at Westminster—was dissolved, and a
new one elected (1774), when he was once again returned
for Middlesex, and took his seat.

The London multitude had grown zealous for Wilkes,
and the town had been harassed by disorder. Of the
fierce brutality of the crowd of that age, we may form a
vivid idea from the unflinching pencil of Hogarth. Barbarous laws were cruelly administered. The common people were turbulent, because misrule made them miserable.
Wilkes had written filthy verses, but the crowd cared no
more for this than their betters cared about the vices of
Lord Sandwich. They made common cause with one who
was accidentally a more conspicuous sufferer. Wilkes was
quite right when he vowed that he was no Wilkite. The
masses were better than their leader. " Whenever the
people have a feeling," Burke once said, " they commonly
are in the right: they sometimes mistake the physician."
Franklin, who was then in London, was of opinion that if
George III. had had a bad character, and John Wilkes a
good one, the latter might have turned the former out of
the kingdom ; for the turbulence that began in street riots
at one time threatened to end in revolt. The King
himself was attacked with savage invective in papers of
which it was said, that no one in the previous century
would have dared to print any like them until Charles was
fast locked up in Carisbrooke Castle.

As is usual when the minds of those in power have
been infected with an arbitrary temper, the employment
of military force to crush civil disturbances became a familiar and favourite idea. The military, said Lord Wey-
mouth, in an elaborate letter which he addressed to the
Surrey magistrates, can never be employed to a more con-

stitutional purpose than in the support of the authority
and dignity of the magistracy. If the magistrate should
be menaced, he is cautioned not to delay a moment in
calling for the aid of the military, and making use of
them effectually. The consequence of this bloody scroll,
as Wilkes rightly called it, was that shortly afterwards
an affray occurred between the crowd and the troops, in
which some twenty people were killed and wounded (May
10, 1768). On the following day, the Secretary of War,
Lord Barrington, wrote to the commanding officer, informing him that the King highly approved of the conduct
both of officers and men, and wished that his gracious ap-
probation of them should be communicated to them.

Burke brought the matter before the House in a motion
for a Committee of Inquiry, supported by one of the most
lucid and able of his minor speeches. "If ever the time
should come," he concluded, "when this House shall be
found prompt to execute and slow to inquire; ready to
punish the excesses of the people, and slow to listen to
their grievances; ready to grant supplies, and slow to examine the account; ready to invest magistrates with large
powers, and slow to inquire into the exercise of them;
ready to entertain notions of the military power as incor-
porated with the constitution—when you learn this in the
air of St. James's, then the business is done; then the
House of Commons will change that character which it
receives from the people only." It is hardly necessary to
say that his motion for a committee was lost by the overwhelming majority of two hundred and forty-five against
thirty. The general result of the proceedings of the government from the accession of George III. to the beginning
of the troubles in the American colonies, was in Burke's
own words, that the government was at once dreaded and

contemned; that the laws were despoiled of all their respected and salutary terrors; that their inaction was a subject of ridicule, and their exertion of abhorrence; that our
dependencies had slackened in their affections; that we
knew neither how to yield nor how to enforce; and that
disconnection and confusion, in offices, in parties, in families, in Parliament, in the nation, prevailed beyond the disorders of any former time.

It was in the pamphlet on the *Present Discontents*, published in 1770, that Burke dealt at large with the whole
scheme of policy of which all these irregularities were the
distempered incidents. The pamphlet was composed as a
manifesto of the Rockingham section of the Whig party,
to show, as Burke wrote to his chief, how different it was
in spirit and composition from "the Bedfords, the Gren-
villes, and other knots, who are combined for no public
purpose, but only as a means of furthering with joint
strength their private and individual advantage." The
pamphlet was submitted in manuscript or proof to the
heads of the party. Friendly critics excused some inele-
gancies which they thought they found in occasional passages, by taking for granted, as was true, that he had admitted insertions from other hands. Here for the first
time he exhibited, on a conspicuous scale, the strongest
qualities of his understanding. Contemporaries had an
opportunity of measuring this strength, by comparison
with another performance of similar scope. The letters
of Junius had startled the world the year before. Burke
was universally suspected of being their author, and the
suspicion never wholly died out so long as he lived. There
was no real ground for it beyond the two unconnected
facts, that the letters were powerful letters, and that Burke
had a powerful intellect. Dr. Johnson admitted that he

had never had a better reason for believing that Burke
was Junius, than that he knew nobody else who had the
ability of Junius.   But Johnson discharged his mind of
the thought, at the instant that Burke voluntarily assured
him that he neither wrote the letters of Junius nor knew
who had written them.   The subjects and aim of those
famous pieces were not very different from Burke's tract,
but any one who in our time turns from the letters to the
tract will wonder how the author of the one could ever
have been suspected of writing the other.   Junius is never
more than a railer, and very often he is third-rate even as
a railer.   The author of the *Present Discontents* speaks
without bitterness even of Lord Bute and the Duke of
Grafton ; he only refers to persons, when their conduct or
their situation illustrates a principle.   Instead of reviling,
he probes, he reflects, he warns ; and as the result of this
serious method, pursued by a man in whom close mastery
of detail kept exact pace with wide grasp of generalities,
we have not the ephemeral diatribe of a faction, but one
of the monumental pieces of political literature.

The last great pamphlet in the history of English public affairs had been Swift's tract *On the Conduct of the
Allies* (1711), in which the writer did a more substantial
service for the Tory party of his day than Burke did for
the Whig party of a later date.   Swift's pamphlet is close,
strenuous, persuasive, and full of telling strokes ; but nobody need read it to-day, except the historical student, or
a member of the Peace Society, in search of the most
convincing exposure of the most insane of English wars.[1]
There is not a sentence in it which does not belong exclusively to the matter in hand : not a line of that general

[1] This was not Burke's judgment on the long war against Louis
XIV.   See *Regicide Peace*, i.

wisdom which is for all time. In the *Present Discontents*
the method is just the opposite of this. The details are
slurred, and they are not literal. Burke describes with
excess of elaboration how the new system is a system of
double cabinets; one put forward with nominal powers in
Parliament, the other concealed behind the throne, and secretly dictating the policy. The reader feels that this is
worked out far too closely to be real. It is a structure of
artificial rhetoric. But we lightly pass this over, on our
way to more solid matter; to the exposition of the principles of a constitution, the right methods of statesmanship, and the defence of party.

It was Bolingbroke, and not Swift, of whom Burke was
thinking, when he sat down to the composition of his
tract. The *Patriot King* was the fountain of the new
doctrines, which Burke trained his party to understand
and to resist. If his foe was domestic, it was from a foreign armoury that Burke derived the instruments of resistance. The great fault of political writers is their too
close adherence to the forms of the system of state which
they happen to be expounding or examining. They stop
short at the anatomy of institutions, and do not penetrate
to the secret of their functions. An illustrious author
in the middle of the eighteenth century introduced his
contemporaries to a better way. It is not too much to
say that at that epoch the strength of political speculation in this country, from Adam Smith downwards, was
drawn from France; and Burke had been led to some of
what was most characteristic in his philosophy of society
by Montesquieu's *Spirit of Laws* (1748), the first great
manual of the historic school. We have no space here to
work out the relations between Montesquieu's principles
and Burke's, but the student of the *Esprit des Lois* will

recognize its influence in every one of Burke's masterpieces.

So far as immediate events were concerned, Burke was
quick to discern their true interpretation. As has been
already said, he attributed to the King and his party a
deliberateness of system which probably had no real existence in their minds. The King intended to reassert
the old right of choosing his own ministers. George II.
had made strenuous but futile endeavours to the same
end. His son, the father of George III., Frederick, Prince
of Wales, as every reader of Dodington's Diary will remember, was equally bent on throwing off the yoke of the
great Whig combinations, and making his own cabinets.
George III. was only continuing the purpose of his father
and his grandfather; and there is no reason to believe
that he went more elaborately to work to obtain his ends.

It is when he leaves the artifices of a cabal, and strikes
down below the surface to the working of deep social
forces, that we feel the breadth and power of Burke's
method. "I am not one of those," he began, "who
think that the people are never wrong. They have been
so, frequently and outrageously, both in other countries
and in this. But I do say that *in all disputes between
them and their rulers, the presumption is at least upon a
par in favour of the people.*" Nay, experience perhaps
justifies him in going further. When popular discontents
are prevalent, something has generally been found amiss
in the constitution or the administration. "The people
have no interest in disorder. When they go wrong, it is
their error, and not their crime." And then he quotes the
famous passage from the Memoirs of Sully, which both
practical politicians and political students should bind
about their necks, and write upon the tables of their

3*

hearts: "The revolutions that come to pass in great states are not the result of chance, nor of popular caprice. . . . As for the populace, it is never from a passion for attack that it rebels, but from impatience of suffering."

What really gives its distinction to the *Present Discontents* is not its plea for indulgence to popular impatience, nor its plea for the superiority of government by aristocracy, but rather the presence in it of the thought of Montesquieu and his school, of the necessity of studying political phenomena in relation, not merely to forms of government and law, but in relation to whole groups of social facts which give to law and government the spirit that makes them workable. Connected with this, is a particularly wide interpretation and a particularly impressive application of the maxims of expediency, because a wide conception of the various interacting elements of a society naturally extends the considerations which a balance of expediencies will include. Hence, in time, there came a strong and lofty ideal of the true statesman, his breadth of vision, his flexibility of temper, his hardly measurable influence. These are the principal thoughts in the *Discontents* to which that tract owes its permanent interest. "Whatever original energy," says Burke, in one place, "may be supposed either in force or regulation, the operation of both is in truth merely instrumental. Nations are governed by the same methods, and on the same principles, by which an individual without authority is often able to govern those who are his equals or superiors; by a knowledge of their temper, and by a judicious management of it. . . . The laws reach but a very little way. Constitute Government how you please, infinitely the greater part of it must depend upon the exercise of powers, which are left at large to the prudence and upright-

ness of ministers of state. Even all the use and potency
of the laws depends upon them. Without them, your
Commonwealth is no better than *a scheme upon paper;
and not a living, active, effective constitution.*" Thus early
in his public career had Burke seized that great antithe-
sis which he so eloquently laboured in the long and ever
memorable episode of his war against the French Revolution : the opposition between artificial arrangements in
politics, and a living, active, effective organization, formed
by what he calls elsewhere in the present tract, the natural
strength of the kingdom, and suitable to the temper and
mental habits of the people. When he spoke of the natural strength of the kingdom, he gave no narrow or conventional account of it. He included in the elements of
that strength, besides the great peers and the leading land-
ed gentlemen, the opulent merchants and manufacturers,
and the substantial yeomanry. Contrasted with the trite
versions of government as fixed in King, Lords, and Commons, this search for the real organs of power was going
to the root of the matter in a spirit at once thoroughly
scientific and thoroughly practical. Burke had, by the
speculative training to which he had submitted himself
in dealing with Bolingbroke, prepared his mind for a
complete grasp of the idea of the body politic as a complex growth, a manifold whole, with closely interdepend-
ent relations among its several parts and divisions. It
was this conception from which his conservatism sprang.
Revolutionary politics have one of their sources in the
idea that societies are capable of infinite and immediate
modifications, without reference to the deep-rooted conditions that have worked themselves into every part of the
social structure.

The same opposition of the positive to the doctrinaire

spirit is to be observed in the remarkable vindication of
Party, which fills the last dozen pages of the pamphlet,
and which is one of the most courageous of all Burke's
deliverances. Party combination is exactly one of those
contrivances which, as it might seem, a wise man would
accept for working purposes, but about which he would
take care to say as little as possible. There appears to be
something revolting to the intellectual integrity and self-
respect of the individual, in the systematic surrender of
his personal action, interest, and power, to a political connexion in which his own judgment may never once be
allowed to count for anything. It is like the surrender
of the right of private judgment to the authority of the
Church, but with its nakedness not concealed by a mystic
doctrine. Nothing is more easy to demolish by the bare
logical reason. But Burke cared nothing about the bare
logical reason, until it had been clothed in convenience
and custom, in the affections on one side, and experience
on the other. Not content with insisting that for some
special purpose of the hour, " when bad men combine, the
good must associate," he contended boldly for the merits
of fidelity to party combination in itself. Although Burke
wrote these strong pages as a reply to Bolingbroke, who
had denounced party as an evil, they remain as the best
general apology that has ever been offered for that principle of public action, against more philosophic attacks
than Bolingbroke's. Burke admitted that when he saw a
man acting a desultory and disconnected part in public
life with detriment to his fortune, he was ready to believe
such a man to be in earnest, though not ready to believe
him to be right. In any case he lamented to see rare
and valuable qualities squandered away without any public
utility. He admitted, moreover, on the other hand, that

people frequently acquired in party confederacies a narrow, bigoted, and proscriptive spirit. "But where duty renders a critical situation a necessary one, it is our business to keep free from the evils attendant upon it, and not to fly from the situation itself. It is surely no very rational account of a man that he has always acted right; but has taken special care to act in such a manner that his endeavours could not possibly be productive of any consequence. . . . When men are not acquainted with each other's principles, nor experienced in each other's talents, nor at all practised in their mutual habitudes and dispositions by joint efforts of business; no personal confidence, no friendship, no common interest subsisting among them; it is evidently impossible that they can act a public part with uniformity, perseverance, or efficacy."

In terms of eloquent eulogy he praised the sacred reverence with which the Romans used to regard the *necessitudo sortis*, or the relations that grew up between men who had only held office together by the casual fortune of the lot. He pointed out to emulation the Whig junto who held so close together in the reign of Anne—Sunderland, Godolphin, Somers, and Marlborough—who believed "that no men could act with effect who did not act in concert; that no men could act in concert who did not act with confidence; and that no men could act with confidence who were not bound together by common opinions, common affections, and common interests." In reading these energetic passages we have to remember two things: first, that the writer assumes the direct object of party combination to be generous, great, and liberal causes; and, second, that when the time came, and when he believed that his friends were espousing a wrong and pernicious cause, Burke, like Samson bursting asunder the

seven green withes, broke away from the friendships of a
life, and deliberately broke his party in pieces.[1]

When Burke came to discuss the cure for the disorders
of 1770, he insisted on contenting himself with what he
ought to have known to be obviously inadequate prescriptions.   And we cannot help feeling that he never speaks
of the constitution of the government of this country
without gliding into a fallacy identical with that which he
himself described and denounced, as thinking better of the
wisdom and power of human legislation than in truth it
deserved.   He was uniformly consistent in his view of
the remedies which the various sections of Opposition proposed against the existing debasement and servility of the
Lower House.   The Duke of Richmond wanted universal
suffrage, equal electoral districts, and annual parliaments.
Wilkes proposed to disfranchise the rotten boroughs, to
increase the county constituencies, and to give members
to rich, populous, trading towns—a general policy which
was accepted fifty - six years afterwards.   The Constitutional Society desired frequent parliaments, the exclusion
of placemen from the House, and the increase of the county representation.   Burke uniformly refused to give his
countenance to any proposals such as these, which involved
a clearly organic change in the constitution.   He confessed
that he had no sort of reliance upon either a triennial parliament or a place-bill, and with that reasonableness which
as a rule was fully as remarkable in him as his eloquence,
he showed very good grounds for his want of faith in the
popular specifics.   In truth, triennial or annual parliaments could have done no good, unless the change had
been accompanied by the more important process of
amputating, as Chatham called it, the rotten boroughs.

[1] See on the same subject, *Corresp.* ii. 276–7.

Of these the Crown could at that time reckon some seventy as its own property. Besides those which belonged to the Crown, there was also the immense number which belonged to the Peerage. If the King sought to strengthen an administration, the thing needful was not to enlist the services of able and distinguished men, but to conciliate a duke, who brought with him the control of a given quantity of voting power in the Lower House. All this patrician influence, which may be found at the bottom of most of the intrigues of the period, would not have been touched by curtailing the duration of parliaments.

What then was the remedy, or had Burke no remedy to offer for these grave distempers of Parliament? Only the remedy of the interposition of the body of the people itself. We must beware of interpreting this phrase in the modern democratic sense. In 1766 he had deliberately declared that he thought it would be more conformable to the spirit of the constitution, "by lessening the number, to add to the weight and independency of our voters." "Considering the immense and dangerous charge of elections, the prostitute and daring venality, the corruption of manners, the idleness and profligacy of the lower sort of voters, no prudent man would propose to increase such an evil."[1] In another place he denies that the people have either enough of speculation in the closet, or of experience in business, to be competent judges, not of the detail of particular measures only, but of *general schemes of policy*.[2] On Burke's theory, the people, as a rule, were no more concerned to interfere with Parliament, than a man is concerned to interfere with somebody whom he has voluntarily and deliberately made his trustee. But here, he con-

---

[1] *Observations on late State of the Nation*, Works, i. 105, b.
[2] *Speech on Duration of Parliaments.*

fessed, was a shameful and ruinous breach of trust.   The
ordinary rule of government was being every day mis-
chievously contemned and daringly set aside.   Until the
confidence thus outraged should be once more restored,
then the people ought to be excited to a more strict and
detailed attention to the conduct of their representatives.
The meetings of counties and corporations ought to settle
standards for judging more systematically of the behaviour of those whom they had sent to Parliament.   Frequent and correct lists of the voters in all important questions ought to be procured.   The severest discouragement
ought to be given to the pernicious practice of affording a
blind and undistinguishing support to every administration.   "Parliamentary support comes and goes with office,
totally regardless of the man or the merit."   For instance,
Wilkes's annual motion to expunge the votes upon the
Middlesex election had been uniformly rejected, as often
as it was made while Lord North was in power.   Lord
North had no sooner given way to the Rockingham Cabinet, than the House of Commons changed its mind, and
the resolutions were expunged by a handsome majority of
115 to 47.   Administration was omnipotent in the House,
because it could be a man's most efficient friend at an
election, and could most amply reward his fidelity afterwards.   Against this system Burke called on the nation
to set a stern face.   Root it up, he kept crying; settle the
general course in which you desire members to go; insist
that they shall not suffer themselves to be diverted from
this by the authority of the government of the day; let
lists of votes be published, so that you may ascertain for
yourselves whether your trustees have been faithful or
fraudulent; do all this, and there will be no need to resort to those organic changes, those empirical innovations,

which may possibly cure, but are much more likely to destroy.

It is not surprising that so halting a policy should have given deep displeasure to very many, perhaps to most, of those whose only common bond was the loose and negative sentiment of antipathy to the court, the ministry, and the too servile majority of the House of Commons. The Constitutional Society was furious. Lord Chatham wrote to Lord Rockingham that the work in which these doctrines first appeared must do much mischief to the common cause. But Burke's view of the constitution was a part of his belief with which he never paltered, and on which he surrendered his judgment to no man. "Our constitution," in his opinion, "stands on a nice equipoise, with steep precipices and deep waters upon all sides of it. In removing it from a dangerous leaning towards one side, there may be a risk of oversetting it on the other."[1] This image was ever before his mind. It occurs again in the last sentence of that great protest against all change and movement, when he describes himself as one who, when the equipoise of the vessel in which he sails may be endangered by overloading it upon one side, is desirous of carrying the small weight of his reasons to that which may preserve its equipoise.[2] When we think of the odious misgovernment in England which the constitution permitted, between the time when Burke wrote and the passing of Lord Sidmouth's Six Acts fifty years later, we may be inclined to class such a constitution among the most inadequate and mischievous political arrangements that any free country has ever had to endure. Yet it was this which Burke declared that he looked upon with filial

[1] *Present Discontents.*
[2] *Reflections on the French Revolution.*

reverence. "Never will I cut it in pieces, and put it into
the kettle of any magician, in order to boil it with the pud-
dle of their compounds into youth and vigour; on the contrary, I will drive away such pretenders; I will nurse its venerable age, and with lenient arts extend a parent's breath."

He was filled with the spirit, and he borrowed the arguments, which have always marked the champion of faith
and authority against the impious assault of reason or innovation.   The constitution was sacred to him as the voice
of the Church and the oracles of her saints are sacred to
the faithful.   Study it, he cried, until you know how to
admire it, and if you cannot know and admire, rather believe that you are dull, than that the rest of the world has
been imposed upon.   We ought to understand it according to our measure, and to venerate where we are not able
presently to comprehend.   Well has Burke been called the
Bossuet of politics.

Although, however, Burke's unflinching reverence for
the constitution, and his reluctance to lay a finger upon it,
may now seem clearly excessive, as it did to Chatham and
his son, who were great men in the right, or to Beckford
and Sawbridge, who were very little men in the right, we
can only be just to him by comparing his ideas with those
which were dominant throughout an evil reign.   While
he opposed more frequent parliaments, he still upheld
the doctrine that "to govern according to the sense, and
agreeably to the interests, of the people is a great and glorious object of government."   While he declared himself
against the addition of a hundred knights of the shire, he
in the very same breath protested that, though the people
might be deceived in their choice of an object, he "could
scarcely conceive any choice they could make, to be so
very mischievous as the existence of any human force ca-

pable of resisting it."[1]   To us this may seem very mild
and commonplace doctrine, but it was not commonplace
in an age when Anglican divines — men like Archbishop
Markham, Dr. Nowell, or Dr. Porteous — had revived the
base precepts of passive obedience and non-resistance, and
when such a man as Lord Mansfield encouraged them.
And these were the kind of foundations which Burke had
been laying, while Fox was yet a Tory, while Sheridan was
writing farces, and while Grey was a schoolboy.

It is, however, almost demonstrably certain that the vindication of the supremacy of popular interests over all other considerations would have been bootless toil, and that
the great constitutional struggle from 1760 to 1783 would
have ended otherwise than it did, but for the failure of the
war against the insurgent colonies, and the final establishment of American Independence.   It was this portentous
transaction which finally routed the arbitrary and despotic
pretensions of the House of Commons over the people,
and which put an end to the hopes entertained by the sovereign of making his personal will supreme in the Chambers.   Fox might well talk of an early Loyalist victory
in the war, as the terrible news from Long Island.   The
struggle which began unsuccessfully at Brentford in Middlesex, was continued at Boston in Massachusetts.   The
scene had changed, but the conflicting principles were the
same.   The war of Independence was virtually a second
English civil war.   The ruin of the American cause would
have been also the ruin of the constitutional cause in England ; and a patriotic Englishman may revere the memory
of Patrick Henry and George Washington not less justly than the patriotic American.   Burke's attitude in this
great contest is that part of his history about the majestic
and noble wisdom of which there can be least dispute.

[1] *To the Chairman of the Buckinghamshire Meeting*. 1780.

CHAPTER IV.

THE ROCKINGHAM PARTY—PARIS—ELECTION AT BRISTOL—
THE AMERICAN WAR.

THE war with the American colonies was preceded by an interval of stupor. The violent ferment which had been stirred in the nation by the affairs of Wilkes and the Middlesex election was followed, as Burke said, by as remarkable a deadness and vapidity. In 1770 the distracted ministry of the Duke of Grafton came to an end, and was succeeded by that of Lord North. The King had at last triumphed. He had secured an administration of which the fundamental principle was that the sovereign was to be the virtual head of it, and the real director of its counsels. Lord North's government lasted for twelve years, and its career is for ever associated with one of the most momentous chapters in the history of the English nation and of free institutions.

Through this long and eventful period, Burke's was as the voice of one crying in the wilderness. He had become important enough for the ministry to think it worth while to take pains to discredit him. They busily encouraged the report that he was Junius, or a close ally to Junius. This was one of the minor vexations of Burke's middle life. Even his friends continued to torment him for incessant disclaimers. Burke's lofty pride made him slow to deal positively with what he scorned as a malicious and

unworthy imputation. To such a friend as Johnson he
did not, as we have seen, disdain to volunteer a denial, but
Charles Townshend was forced to write more than one importunate letter before he could extract from Burke the
definite sentence (Nov. 24, 1771) : " I now give you my
word and honour that I am not the author of Junius, and
that I know not the author of that paper, and I do author-
ize you to say so." Nor was this the only kind of annoy-
ance to which he was subjected. His rising fame kindled
the candour of the friends of his youth. With proverbial
good - nature, they admonished him that he did not bear
instruction ; that he showed such arrogance as in a man
of his condition was intolerable ; that he snapped furious-
ly at his parliamentary foes, like a wolf who had broken
into the fold ; that his speeches were useless declamations ;
and that he disgraced the House by the scurrilities of the
bear-garden. These sharp chastenings of friendship Burke
endured with the perfect self - command, not of the cold
and indifferent egotist, but of one who had trained himself
not to expect too much from men. He possessed the true
solace for all private chagrins in the activity and the fervour of his public interests.

In 1772 the affairs of the East India Company, and its
relations with the Government, had fallen into disorder.
The Opposition, though powerless in the Houses of Parliament, were often able to thwart the views of the ministry in the imperial board-room in Leadenhall Street. The
Duke of Richmond was as zealous and as active in his opposition to Lord North in the business of the East Indies
as he was in the business of the country at Westminster.
A proposal was made to Burke to go out to India at the
head of a commission of three supervisors, with authority
to examine the concerns of every department, and full

powers of control over the company's servants. Though this offer was pressed by the directors, Burke, after anxious consideration, declined it. What his reasons were, there is no evidence; we can only guess that he thought less of his personal interests than of those of the country and of his party. Without him the Rockingham connexion would undoubtedly have fallen to ruin, and with it the most upright, consistent, and disinterested body of men then in public life. " You say," the Duke of Richmond wrote to him (Nov. 15, 1772), " the party is an object of too much importance to go to pieces. Indeed, Burke, you have more merit than any man in keeping us together." It was the character of the party, almost as much as their principles, that secured Burke's zeal and attachment; their decorum, their constancy, their aversion to all cabals for private objects, their indifference to office, except as an instrument of power and a means of carrying out the policy of their convictions. They might easily have had office, if they would have come in upon the King's terms. A year after his fall from power, Lord Rockingham was summoned to the royal closet, and pressed to resume his post. But office at any price was not in their thoughts. They knew the penalties of their system, and they clung to it undeterred. Their patriotism was deliberate and considered. Chalcedon was called the city of the blind, because its founders wilfully neglected the more glorious site of Byzantium which lay under their eyes. " We have built our Chalcedon," said Burke, " with the chosen part of the universe full in our prospect." They had the faults to which an aristocratic party in opposition is naturally liable. Burke used to reproach them with being somewhat languid, scrupulous, and unsystematic. He could not make the Duke of Richmond put off a large party at Goodwood for the sake of an important division in the House of Lords; and he did not always agree with Lord John Cavendish as to what constitutes a decent and reasonable quantity of fox-hunting for a political leader in a crisis. But it was part of the steadfastness of his whole life to do his best with such materials as he could find ; he did not lose patience nor abate his effort, because his friends would miss the opportunity of a great political stroke, rather than they would miss Newmarket Races. He wrote their protests for the House of Lords, composed petitions for county meetings, drafted resolutions, and plied them with information, ideas, admonitions, and exhortations. Never before nor since has our country seen so extraordinary a union of the clever and indefatigable party-manager, with the reflective and philosophic habits of the speculative publicist. It is much easier to make either absolutism or democracy attractive than aristocracy ; yet we see how consistent with his deep moral conservatism was Burke's attachment to an aristocratic party, when we read his exhortation to the Duke of Richmond to remember that persons in his high station of life ought to have long views. "You people," he writes to the Duke (November 17, 1772), " of great families and hereditary trusts and fortunes, are not like such as I am, who, whatever we may be, by the rapidity of our growth, and even by the fruit we bear, and flatter ourselves that, while we creep on the ground, we belly into melons that are exquisite for size and flavour, yet still we are but annual plants that perish with our season, and leave no sort of traces behind us. You, if you are what you ought to be, are in my eye the great oaks that shade a country, and perpetuate your benefits from generation to generation. The immediate power of a Duke of Richmond, or a Marquis of Rockingham,

is not so much of moment; but if their conduct and example hand down their principles to their successors, then
their houses become the public repositories and office of
record for the constitution. . . . I do not look upon your
time or lives as lost, if in this sliding away from the genuine spirit of the country, certain parties, if possible—if not,
the heads of certain families—should make it their business by the whole course of their lives, principally by their
example, to mould into the very vital stamina of their descendants, those principles which ought to be transmitted
pure and unmixed to posterity."

Perhaps such a passage as this ought to be described
less as reflection than as imagination—moral, historic, conservative imagination—in which order, social continuity,
and the endless projection of past into present, and of present into future, are clothed with the sanctity of an inner
shrine. We may think that a fox-hunting duke and a
racing marquis were very poor centres round which to
group these high emotions. But Burke had no puny sentimentalism, and none of the mere literary or romantic
conservatism of men like Chateaubriand. He lived in the
real world, and not in a false dream of some past world
that had never been. He saw that the sporting squires of
his party were as much the representatives of ancestral
force and quality, as in older days were long lines of
Claudii and Valerii. His conservative doctrine was a profound instinct, in part political, but in greater part moral.
The accidental roughness of the symbol did not touch him,
for the symbol was glorified by the sincerity of his faith
and the compass of his imagination.

With these ideas strong within him, in 1773 Burke
made a journey to France. It was almost as though the
solemn hierophant of some mystic Egyptian temple should

have found himself amid the brilliant chatter of a band
of reckless, keen-tongued disputants of the garden or the
porch at Athens. His only son had just finished a successful school-course at Westminster, and was now entered
a student at Christ Church. He was still too young for
the university, and Burke thought that a year could not
be more profitably spent than in forming his tongue to
foreign languages. The boy was placed at Auxerre, in the
house of the business agent of the Bishop of Auxerre.
From the Bishop he received many kindnesses, to be amply repaid in after-years when the Bishop came in his old
age, an exile and a beggar, to England.

While in Paris, Burke did all that he could to instruct
himself as to what was going on in French society. If he
had not the dazzling reception which had greeted Hume
in 1764, at least he had ample opportunities of acquaint-
ing himself with the prevailing ideas of the times, in more
than one of the social camps into which Paris was then
divided. Madame du Deffand tells the Duchess of Choi-
seul that though he speaks French extremely ill, everybody
felt that he would be infinitely agreeable if he could more
easily make himself understood. He followed French well
enough as a listener, and went every day to the courts to
hear the barristers and watch the procedure. Madame du
Deffand showed him all possible attention, and her friends
eagerly seconded her. She invited him to supper parties
where he met the Count de Broglie, the agent of the king's
secret diplomacy; Caraccioli, successor of the nimble-wit-
ted Galiani as minister from Naples; and other notabilities
of the high world. He supped with the Duchess of Lux-
embourg, and heard a reading of La Harpe's *Barmecides*.
It was high treason in this circle to frequent the rival salon
of Mademoiselle Lespinasse, but either the law was relaxed

4

in the case of foreigners, or else Burke kept his own counsel. Here were for the moment the headquarters of the
party of innovation, and here he saw some of the men who
were busily forging the thunderbolts. His eye was on the
alert, now as always, for anything that might light up the
sovereign problems of human government. A book, by a
member of this circle, had appeared six months before,
which was still the talk of the town, and against which the
government had taken the usual impotent measures of repression. This was the *Treatise on Tactics*, by a certain
M. de Guibert, a colonel of the Corsican legion. The important part of the work was the introduction, in which
the writer examined with what was then thought extraordinary hardihood, the social and political causes of the decline of the military art in France. Burke read it with
keen interest and energetic approval. He was present at
the reading of a tragedy by the same author, and gave
some offence to the rival coterie by preferring Guibert's
tragedy to La Harpe's. To us, however, of a later day,
Guibert is known neither for his tragedy nor his essay on
tactics, nor for a memory so rapid that he could open a
book, throw one glance like a flash of lightning on to a
page, and then instantly repeat from it half a dozen lines
word for word. He lives in literature as the inspirer of
that ardent passion of Mademoiselle Lespinasse's letters, so
unique in their consuming intensity that, as has been said,
they seem to burn the page on which they are written. It
was, perhaps, at Mademoiselle Lespinasse's that Burke met
Diderot. The eleven volumes of the illustrative plates of
the Encyclopædia had been given to the public twelve
months before, and its editor was just released from the
giant's toil of twenty years. Voltaire was in imperial exile
at Ferney. Rousseau was copying music in a garret in the

street which is now called after his name, but he had long
ago cut himself off from society; and Burke was not likely to take much trouble to find out a man whom he had
known in England seven years before, and against whom
he had conceived a strong and lasting antipathy, as enter-
taining no principle either to influence his heart or to
guide his understanding save a deranged and eccentric
vanity.

It was the fashion for English visitors to go to Versailles.
They saw the dauphin and his brothers dine in public, before a crowd of princes of the blood, nobles, abbés, and all
the miscellaneous throng of a court.   They attended mass
in the chapel, where the old King, surrounded by bishops,
sat in a pew just above that of Madame du Barri.   The
royal mistress astonished foreigners by hair without pow-
der and cheeks without rouge, the simplest toilettes, and
the most unassuming manners.   Vice itself, in Burke's
famous words, seemed to lose half its evil by losing all its
grossness.   And there, too, Burke had that vision to which
we owe one of the most gorgeous pages in our literature—
Marie Antoinette, the young dauphiness, "decorating and
cheering the elevated sphere she just began to move in,
glittering like the morning-star, full of life and splendour
and joy."   The shadow was rapidly stealing on.   The
year after Burke's visit, the scene underwent a strange
transformation.   The King died; the mistress was banished in luxurious exile; and the dauphiness became the
ill-starred Queen of France.   Burke never forgot the emotions of the scene; they awoke in his imagination sixteen
years after, when all was changed, and the awful contrast
shook him with a passion that his eloquence has made
immortal.

Madame du Deffand wrote to Horace Walpole that

Burke had been so well received, that he ought to leave
France excellently pleased with the country. But it was
not so. His spirit was perturbed by what he had listened
to. He came away with small esteem for that busy fer-
mentation of intellect in which his French friends most
exulted, and for which they looked forward to the gratitude and admiration of posterity. From the spot on
which he stood there issued two mighty streams. It was
from the ideas of the Parisian Freethinkers whom Burke
so detested, that Jefferson, Franklin, and Henry drew those
theories of human society which were so soon to find life
in American Independence. It was from the same ideas
that later on that revolutionary tide surged forth, in which
Burke saw no elements of a blessed fertility, but only a
horrid torrent of red and desolating lava. In 1773 there
was a moment of strange repose in Western Europe, the
little break of stillness that precedes the hurricane. It
was, indeed, the eve of a momentous epoch. Before sixteen years were over, the American Republic had risen like
a new constellation into the firmament, and the French
monarchy, of such antiquity and fame and high pre-emi-
nence in European history, had been shattered to the dust.
We may not agree with Burke's appreciation of the forces
that were behind these vast convulsions. But at least he
saw, and saw with eyes of passionate alarm, that strong
speculative forces were at work, which must violently
prove the very bases of the great social superstructure,
and might not improbably break them up for ever.

Almost immediately after his return from France, he
sounded a shrill note of warning. Some Methodists from
Chatham had petitioned Parliament against a bill for
the relief of Dissenters from subscription to the Articles.
Burke denounced the intolerance of the petitioners. It is

not the Dissenters, he cried, whom you have to fear, but
the men who, "not contented with endeavouring to turn
your eyes from the blaze and effulgence of light, by which
life and immortality is so gloriously demonstrated by the
Gospel, would even extinguish that faint glimmering of
Nature, that only comfort supplied to ignorant man before
this great illumination. . . . These are the people against
whom you ought to aim the shaft of the law; these are
the men to whom, arrayed in all the terrors of government,
I would say, 'You shall not degrade us into brutes.' . . .
The most horrid and cruel blow that can be offered to civil
society is through atheism. . . . The infidels are outlaws
of the constitution, not of this country, but of the human
race. They are never, never to be supported, never to be
tolerated. Under the systematic attacks of these people, I
see some of the props of good government already begin
to fail; I see propagated principles which will not leave to
religion even a toleration. I see myself sinking every day
under the attacks of these wretched people."[1] To this
pitch he had been excited by the vehement band of men,
who had inscribed on their standard *Écraser l'Infame*.

The second Parliament in which Burke had a seat was
dissolved suddenly and without warning (October, 1774).
The attitude of America was threatening, and it was believed the Ministers were anxious to have the elections
over before the state of things became worse. The whole
kingdom was instantly in a ferment. Couriers, chaises,
post-horses hurried in every direction over the island, and
it was noted, as a measure of the agitation, that no fewer
than sixty messengers passed through a single turnpike on
one day. Sensible observers were glad to think that, in

[1] *Speech on Relief of Protestant Dissenters*, 1773.

consequence of the rapidity of the elections, less wine and
money would be wasted than at any election for sixty
years past.   Burke had a houseful of company at Beaconsfield when the news arrived.   Johnson was among them,
and as the party was hastily breaking up, the old Tory
took his Whig friend kindly by the hand : "Farewell, my
dear sir," he said, "and remember that I wish you all the
success that ought to be wished to you, and can possibly
be wished to you, by an honest man."

The words were of good omen.   Burke was now re-
warded by the discovery that his labours had earned for
him recognition and gratitude beyond the narrow limits
of a rather exclusive party.   He had before this attracted
the attention of the mercantile public.   The Company of
Merchants trading to Africa voted him their thanks for his
share in supporting their establishments.   The Committee
of Trade at Manchester formally returned him their grate-
ful acknowledgments for the active part that he had taken
in the business of the Jamaica free ports.   But then Manchester returned no representative to Parliament.   In two
Parliaments Burke had been elected for Wendover free of
expense.   Lord Verney's circumstances were now so embarrassed, that he was obliged to part with the four seats
at his disposal to men who could pay for them.   There
had been some talk of proposing Burke for Westminster,
and Wilkes, who was then omnipotent, promised him the
support of the popular party.   But the patriot's memory
was treacherous, and he speedily forgot, for reasons of his
own, an idea that had originated with himself.   Burke's
constancy of spirit was momentarily overclouded.   "Sometimes when I am alone," he wrote to Lord Rockingham
(September 15, 1774), "in spite of all my efforts, I fall
into a melancholy which is inexpressible, and to which, if

I gave way, I should not continue long under it, but must totally sink. Yet I do assure you that partly, and indeed principally, by the force of natural good spirits, and partly by a strong sense of what I ought to do, I bear up so well that no one who did not know them could easily discover the state of my mind or my circumstances. I have those that are dear to me, for whom I must live as long as God pleases, and in what way he pleases. Whether I ought not totally to abandon this public station for which I am so unfit, and have of course been so unfortunate, I know not." But he was always saved from rash retirement from public business by two reflections. He doubted whether a man has a right to retire after he has once gone a certain length in these things. And he remembered that there are often obscure vexations in the most private life, which as effectually destroy a man's peace as anything that can occur in public contentions.

Lord Rockingham offered his influence on behalf of Burke at Malton, one of the family boroughs in Yorkshire, and thither Burke in no high spirits betook himself. On his way to the north he heard that he had been nominated for Bristol, but the nomination had, for certain electioneering reasons, not been approved by the party. As it happened, Burke was no sooner chosen at Malton than, owing to an unexpected turn of affairs at Bristol, the idea of proposing him for a candidate revived. Messengers were sent express to his house in London, and, not finding him there, they hastened down to Yorkshire. Burke quickly resolved that the offer was too important to be rejected. Bristol was the capital of the west, and it was still in wealth, population, and mercantile activity the second city of the kingdom. To be invited to stand for so great a constituency, without any request of his own and free of personal ex-

pense, was a distinction which no politician could hold
lightly. Burke rose from the table where he was dining
with some of his supporters, stepped into a post-chaise at
six on a Tuesday evening, and travelled without a break
until he reached Bristol on the Thursday afternoon, having got over two hundred and seventy miles in forty-four
hours. Not only did he execute the journey without a
break, but, as he told the people of Bristol, with an exult-
ing commemoration of his own zeal that recalls Cicero, he
did not sleep for an instant in the interval. The poll was
kept open for a month, and the contest was the most tedi-
ous that had ever been known in the city. New freemen
were admitted down to the very last day of the election.
At the end of it, Burke was second on the poll, and was
declared to be duly chosen (November 3, 1774). There
was a petition against his return, but the election was confirmed, and he continued to sit for Bristol for six years.

The situation of a candidate is apt to find out a man's
weaker places. Burke stood the test. He showed none
of the petulant rage of those clamorous politicians whose
flight, as he said, is winged in a lower region of the air.
As the traveller stands on the noble bridge that now spans
the valley of the Avon, he may recall Burke's local comparison of these busy, angry familiars of an election, to the
gulls that skim the mud of the river when it is exhausted
of its tide. He gave his new friends a more important
lesson, when the time came for him to thank them for the
honour which they had just conferred upon him. His
colleague had opened the subject of the relations between
a member of Parliament and his constituents; and had
declared that, for his own part, he should regard the instructions of the people of Bristol as decisive and binding.
Burke in a weighty passage upheld a manlier doctrine.

"Certainly, gentlemen, it ought to be the happiness and glory of a representative to live in the strictest union, the closest correspondence, and the most unreserved communication with his constituents. Their wishes ought to have great weight with him; their opinions high respect, their business unremitted attention. It is his duty to sacrifice his repose, his pleasure, his satisfactions, to theirs; and above all, ever, and in all cases, to prefer their interest to his own. But his unbiassed opinion, his mature judgment, his enlightened conscience, he ought not to sacrifice to you, to any man, or to any set of men living. Your representative owes you, not his industry only, but his judgment; and he betrays, instead of serving you, if he sacrifices it to your opinion.

"My worthy colleague says, his will ought to be subservient to yours. If that be all, the thing is innocent. If government were a matter of will upon any side, yours, without question, ought to be superior. But government and legislation are matters of reason and judgment, and not of inclination; and what sort of reason is that in which the determination precedes the discussion, in which one set of men deliberate and another decide, and where those who form the conclusion are perhaps three hundred miles distant from those who hear the arguments? . . . *Authoritative* instructions, *mandates* issued, which the member is bound blindly and implicitly to obey, to vote and to argue for, though contrary to the clearest convictions of his judgment and conscience—these are things utterly unknown to the laws of this land, and which arise from a fundamental mistake of the whole order and tenour of our Constitution."[1]

For six years the British electors were content to be represented by a man of this independence. They never, however, really acquiesced in the principle that a member of Parliament owes as much to his own convictions as to the will of his constituents. In 1778 a bill was brought into Parliament, relaxing some of the restrictions imposed upon Ireland by the atrocious fiscal policy of Great Britain. The great mercantile centres raised a furious outcry, and Bristol was as blind and as boisterous as Manchester

[1] *Speech at the conclusion of the Poll.*

4*

and Glasgow.   Burke not only spoke and voted in favour
of the commercial propositions, but urged that the proposed removal of restrictions on Irish trade did not go
nearly far enough.   There was none of that too familiar
casuistry, by which public men argue themselves out of
their consciences in a strange syllogism, that they can best
serve the country in Parliament; that to keep their seats
they must follow their electors; and that therefore, in the
long run, they serve the country best by acquiescing in ignorance and prejudice.   Anybody can denounce an abuse.
It needs valour and integrity to stand forth against a wrong
to which our best friends are most ardently committed.
It warms our hearts to think of the noble courage with
which Burke faced the blind and vile selfishness of his
own supporters.   He reminded them that England only
consented to leave to the Irish, in two or three instances,
the use of the natural faculties which God had given them.
He asked them whether Ireland was united to Great Britain for no other purpose than that we should counteract
the bounty of Providence in her favour; and whether, in
proportion as that bounty had been liberal, we were to regard it as an evil to be met with every possible corrective?
In our day there is nobody of any school who doubts that
Burke's view of our trade policy towards Ireland was accurately, absolutely, and magnificently right.   I need not
repeat the arguments.   They made no mark on the Bristol merchants.   Burke boldly told them that he would
rather run the risk of displeasing than of injuring them.
They implored him to become their advocate.   "I should
only disgrace myself," he said; "I should lose the only
thing which can make such abilities as mine of any use to
the world now or hereafter.   I mean that authority which
is derived from the opinion that a member speaks the lan-

guage of truth and sincerity, and that he is not ready to take up or lay down a great political system for the convenience of the hour; that he is in Parliament to support his opinion of the public good, and does not form his opinion in order to get into Parliament or to continue in it."[1]

A small instalment of humanity to Ireland was not more distasteful to the electors of Bristol, than a small instalment of toleration to Roman Catholics in England. A measure was passed (1778) repealing certain iniquitous penalties created by an act of William the Third. It is needless to say that this rudimentary concession to justice and sense was supported by Burke. His voters began to believe that those were right who had said that he had been bred at Saint Omer's, was a Papist at heart, and a Jesuit in disguise. When the time came, *summa dies et ineluctabile fatum*, Burke bore with dignity and temper his dismissal from the only independent constituency that he ever represented. Years before he had warned a young man entering public life to regard and wish well to the common people, whom his best instincts and his highest duties lead him to love and to serve, but to put as little trust in them as in princes. Burke somewhere describes an honest public life as carrying on a poor unequal conflict against the passions and prejudices of our day, perhaps with no better weapons than passions and prejudices of our own.

The six years during which Burke sat in Parliament for Bristol saw this conflict carried on under the most desperate circumstances. They were the years of the civil war between the English at home and the English in the American colonies. George III. and Lord North have been made scapegoats for sins which were not exclusively their

[1] *Two letters to gentlemen in Bristol,* 1778.

own. They were only the organs and representatives of
all the lurking ignorance and arbitrary humours of the entire community. Burke discloses in many places, that for
once the King and Parliament did not act without the
sympathies of the mass. In his famous speech at Bristol,
in 1780, he was rebuking the intolerance of those who
bitterly taunted him for the support of the measure for
the relaxation of the Penal Code. " It is but too true,"
he said in a passage worth remembering, " that the love,
and even the very idea, of genuine liberty is extremely
rare. It is but too true that there are many whose whole
scheme of freedom is made up of pride, perverseness, and
insolence. They feel themselves in a state of thraldom;
they imagine that their souls are cooped and cabined in,
unless they have some man, or some body of men, dependent on their mercy. The desire of having some one below
them descends to those who are the very lowest of all;
and a Protestant cobbler, debased by his poverty, but exalted by his share of the ruling church, feels a pride in
knowing it is by his generosity alone that the peer, whose
footman's instep he measures, is able to keep his chaplain
from a gaol. This disposition is the true source of the
passion which many men, in very humble life, have taken
to the American war. *Our* subjects in America; *our*
colonies; *our* dependents. This lust of party power is
the liberty they hunger and thirst for; and this Siren
song of ambition has charmed ears that we would have
thought were never organized to that sort of music."

This was the mental attitude of a majority of the nation,
and it was fortunate for them and for us that the yeomen
and merchants on the other side of the Atlantic had a
more just and energetic appreciation of the crisis. The
insurgents, while achieving their own freedom, were indi-

rectly engaged in fighting the battle of the people of the mother country as well.   Burke had a vehement correspondent who wrote to him (1777) that if the utter ruin of this country were to be the consequence of her persisting in the claim to tax America, then he would be the first to say, *Let her perish!*   If England prevails, said Horace Walpole, English and American liberty is at an end; if one fell, the other would fall with it.   Burke, seeing this, "certainly never could and never did wish," as he says of himself, "the colonists to be subdued by arms.   He was fully persuaded that if such should be the event, they must be held in that subdued state by a great body of standing forces, and perhaps of foreign forces.   He was strongly of opinion that such armies, first victorious over Englishmen, in a conflict for English constitutional rights and privileges, and afterwards habituated (though in America) to keep an English people in a state of abject subjection, would prove fatal in the end to the liberties of England itself."[1]   The way for this remote peril was being sedulously prepared by a widespread deterioration among popular ideas, and a fatal relaxation of the hold which they had previously gained in the public mind.   In order to prove that the Americans had no right to their liberties, we were every day endeavouring to subvert the maxims which preserve the whole spirit of our own.   To prove that the Americans ought not to be free, we were obliged to depreciate the value of freedom itself.   The material strength of the Government, and its moral strength alike, would have been reinforced by the defeat of the colonists, to such an extent as to have seriously delayed or even jeopardized English progress, and therefore that of Europe too.   As events actually fell out, the ferocious administra-

[1] *Appeal from the new to the old Whigs.*

tion of the law in the last five or six years of the eighteenth century, was the retribution for the lethargy or approval with which the mass of the English community had
watched the measures of the government against their fel-
low-Englishmen in America.

It is not necessary here to follow Burke minutely
through the successive stages of parliamentary action in
the American war. He always defended the settlement of
1766 ; the Stamp Act was repealed, and the constitutional
supremacy and sovereign authority of the mother country
was preserved in a Declaratory Act. When the project
of taxing the colonies was revived, and relations with them
were becoming strained and dangerous, Burke came forward with a plan for leaving the General Assemblies of
the colonies to grant supplies and aids, instead of giving
and granting supplies in Parliament, to be raised and paid
in the colonies. Needless to say that it was rejected, and
perhaps it was not feasible. Henceforth Burke could only
watch in impotence the blunders of government, and the
disasters that befell the national arms. But his protests
against the war will last as long as our literature.

Of all Burke's writings none are so fit to secure unqualified and unanimous admiration as the three pieces on this
momentous struggle : the Speech on American Taxation
(April 19, 1774) ; the Speech on Conciliation with America (March 22, 1775) ; and the Letter to the Sheriffs of
Bristol (1777). Together they hardly exceed the compass
of the little volume which the reader now has in his hands.
It is no exaggeration to say that they compose the most
perfect manual in our literature, or in any literature, for
one who approaches the study of public affairs, whether
for knowledge or for practice. They are an example without fault of all the qualities which the critic, whether a

theorist or an actor, of great political situations should
strive by night and by day to possess. If the subject with
which they deal were less near than it is to our interests
and affections as free citizens, these three performances
would still abound in the lessons of an incomparable political method. If their subject were as remote as the quarrel between the Corinthians and Corcyra, or the war between Rome and the Allies, instead of a conflict to which
the world owes the opportunity of the most important of
political experiments, we should still have everything to
learn from the author's treatment; the vigorous grasp of
masses of compressed detail, the wide illumination from
great principles of human experience, the strong and mas-
culine feeling for the two great political ends of Justice
and Freedom, the large and generous interpretation of expediency, the morality, the vision, the noble temper. If
ever, in the fulness of time—and surely the fates of men
and literature cannot have it otherwise—Burke becomes one
of the half-dozen names of established and universal cur-
rency in education and in common books, rising above the
waywardness of literary caprice or intellectual fashions, as
Shakespere and Milton and Bacon rise above it, it will be
the mastery, the elevation, the wisdom, of these far-shining
discourses in which the world will in an especial degree
recognize the combination of sovereign gifts with beneficent uses.

The pamphlet on the *Present Discontents* is partially
obscured or muffled to the modern reader by the space
which is given to the cabal of the day. The *Reflections
on the French Revolution* over-abounds in declamation, and
—apart from its being passionately on one side, and that
perhaps the wrong one—the splendour of the eloquence is
out of proportion to the reason and the judgment. In the

pieces on the American war, on the contrary, Burke was
conscious that he could trust nothing to the sympathy or
the prepossessions of his readers, and this put him upon an
unwonted persuasiveness. Here it is reason and judgment,
not declamation ; lucidity, not passion ; that produces the
effects of eloquence. No choler mars the page ; no purple
patch distracts our minds from the penetrating force of the
argument ; no commonplace is dressed up into a vague sublimity. The cause of freedom is made to wear its own
proper robe of equity, self-control, and reasonableness.

Not one, but all those great idols of the political market-
place whose worship and service has cost the race so dear,
are discovered and shown to be the foolish uncouth stocks
and stones that they are. Fox once urged members of
parliament to peruse the speech on Conciliation again and
again, to study it, to imprint it on their minds, to impress
it on their hearts. But Fox only referred to the lesson
which he thought to be contained in it, that representation is the sovereign remedy for every evil. This is by
far the least important of its lessons. It is great in many
ways. It is greatest as a remonstrance and an answer
against the thriving sophisms of barbarous national pride,
the eternal fallacies of war and conquest ; and here it is
great, as all the three pieces on the subject are so, because
they expose with unanswerable force the deep-lying faults
of heart and temper, as well as of understanding, which
move nations to haughty and violent courses.

The great argument with those of the war party who
pretended to a political defence of their position was the
doctrine that the English government was sovereign in the
colonies as at home ; and in the notion of sovereignty they
found inherent the notion of an indefeasible right to im-
pose and exact taxes. Having satisfied themselves of the

existence of this sovereignty, and of the right which they
took to be its natural property, they saw no step between
the existence of an abstract right and the propriety of en-
forcing it. We have seen an instance of a similar mode of
political thinking in our own lifetime. During the great
civil war between the Northern and Southern States of the
American Union, people in England convinced themselves
—some after careful examination of documents, others by
cursory glances at second-hand authorities—that the South
had a right to secede. The current of opinion was precisely similar in the struggle to which the United States
owed their separate existence. Now the idea of a right as
a mysterious and reverend abstraction, to be worshipped in
a state of naked divorce from expediency and convenience,
was one that Burke's political judgment found preposterous and unendurable. He hated the arbitrary and despotic
savour which clung about the English assumptions over
the colonies. And his repulsion was heightened when he
found that these assumptions were justified, not by some
permanent advantage which their victory would procure
for the mother country or for the colonies, or which would
repay the cost of gaining such a victory ; not by the assertion and demonstration of some positive duty, but by the
futile and meaningless doctrine that we had a right to do
something or other, if we liked.

The alleged compromise of the national dignity implied
in a withdrawal of the just claim of the government, instead of convincing, only exasperated him. "Show the
thing you contend for to be reason; show it to be common-sense ; show it to be the means of attaining some useful end ; and then I am content to allow it what dignity
you please."[1] The next year he took up the ground still

[1] *Speech on American Taxation.*

more firmly, and explained it still more impressively. As
for the question of the right of taxation, he exclaimed,
"It is less than nothing in my consideration. . . . My consideration is narrow, confined, and wholly limited to the
policy of the question. I do not examine whether the
giving away a man's money be a power excepted and reserved out of the general trust of Government. . . . *The
question with me is not whether you have a right to render your people miserable, but whether it is not your interest to make them happy.* It is not what a lawyer tells me
I *may* do, but what humanity, reason, and justice tell me I
ought to do. I am not determining a point of law; I am
restoring tranquillity, and the general character and situation of a people must determine what sort of government
is fitted for them." "I am not here going into the distinctions of rights," he cries, "not attempting to mark
their boundaries. I do not enter into these metaphysical
distinctions. *I hate the very sound of them.* This is the
true touchstone of all theories which regard man and the
affairs of man : does it suit his nature in general ? does it
suit his nature as modified by his habits?" He could not
bear to think of having legislative or political arrangements shaped or vindicated by a delusive geometrical ac-
curacy of deduction, instead of being entrusted to "the
natural operation of things, which, left to themselves, generally fall into their proper order."

Apart from his incessant assertion of the principle that
man acts from adequate motives relative to his interests,
and not on metaphysical speculations, Burke sows, as he
marches along in his stately argument, many a germ of
the modern philosophy of civilization. He was told that
America was worth fighting for. "Certainly it is," he
answered, "if fighting a people be the best way of gaining

them." Every step that has been taken in the direction of progress, not merely in empire, but in education, in punishment, in the treatment of the insane, has shown the deep wisdom, so unfamiliar in that age of ferocious penalties and brutal methods, of this truth—that " the natural effect of fidelity, clemency, kindness in governors, is peace, good-will, order, and esteem in the governed." Is there a single instance to the contrary? Then there is that sure key to wise politics: "*Nobody shall persuade me, when a whole people are concerned, that acts of lenity are not means of conciliation.*" And that still more famous sentence, "*I do not know the method of drawing up an indictment against a whole people.*"

Good and observant men will feel that no misty benevolence or vague sympathy, but the positive reality of experience, inspired such passages as that where he says, "Never expecting to find perfection in men, and not looking for divine attributes in created beings, in my commerce with my contemporaries I have found much human virtue. The age unquestionably produces daring profligates and insidious hypocrites? What then? Am I not to avail myself of whatever good is to be found in the world, because of the mixture of evil that is in it! . . . Those who raise suspicions of the good, on account of the behaviour of evil men, are of the party of the latter. . . . A conscientious person would rather doubt his own judgment, than condemn his species. He that accuses all mankind of corruption, ought to remember that he is sure to convict only one. In truth, I should much rather admit those whom at any time I have disrelished the most, to be patterns of perfection, than seek a consolation to my own unworthiness in a general communion of depravity with all about me." This is one of those pieces of rational

constancy and mental wholeness in Burke, which fill up
our admiration for him—one of the manifold illustrations
of an invincible fidelity to the natural order and operation
of things, even when they seemed most hostile to all that
was dear to his own personality.

CHAPTER V.

ECONOMICAL REFORM — BURKE IN OFFICE — FALL OF HIS
PARTY.

TOWARDS 1780 it began to be clear that the ministers
had brought the country into disaster and humiliation,
from which their policy contained no way of escape. In
the closing months of the American war, the Opposition
pressed ministers with a vigour that never abated. Lord
North bore their attacks with perfect good-humour.
When Burke, in the course of a great oration, parodied
Burgoyne's invitation to the Indians to repair to the
King's standard, the wit and satire of it almost suffo-
cated the prime minister, not with shame but with laugh-
ter. His heart had long ceased to be in the matter, and
everybody knew that he only retained his post in obedience to the urgent importunities of the King, whilst
such colleagues as Rigby only clung to their place because
the salaries were endeared by long familiarity. The general gloom was accidentally deepened by that hideous outbreak of fanaticism and violence, which is known as the
Lord George Gordon Riots (June, 1780). The Whigs, as
having favoured the relaxation of the laws against pop-
ery, were especially obnoxious to the mob. The government sent a guard of soldiers to protect Burke's house in
Charles Street, St. James's; but, after he had removed the
more important of his papers, he insisted on the guard

being dispatched for the protection of more important
places, and he took shelter under the roof of General Burgoyne. His excellent wife, according to a letter of his
brother, had " the firmness and sweetness of an angel ;
but why do I say of an angel ?—of a woman." Burke
himself courageously walked to and fro amid the raging
crowds with firm composure, though the experiment was
full of peril. He describes the mob as being made up, as
London mobs generally are, rather of the unruly and dissolute than of fanatical malignants, and he vehemently
opposed any concessions by Parliament to the spirit of
intolerance which had first kindled the blaze. All the
letters of the time show that the outrages and alarms of
those days and nights, in which the capital seemed to be
at the mercy of a furious rabble, made a deeper impression on the minds of contemporaries than they ought to
have done. Burke was not likely to be less excited than
others by the sight of such insensate disorder; and it is
no idle fancy that he had the mobs of 1780 still in his
memory, when ten years later he poured out the vials of
his wrath on the bloodier mob which carried the King
and Queen of France in wild triumph from Versailles to
Paris.

In the previous February (1780) Burke had achieved
one of the greatest of all his parliamentary and oratorical
successes. Though the matter of this particular enter-
prise is no longer alive, yet it illustrates his many strong
qualities in so remarkable a way that it is right to give
some account of it. We have already seen that Burke
steadily set his face against parliamentary reform ; he habitually declared that the machine was well enough to
answer any good purpose, provided the materials were
sound. The statesman who resists all projects for the

reform of the constitution, and yet eagerly proclaims how
deplorably imperfect are the practical results of its working, binds himself to vigorous exertions for the amend-
ment of administration. Burke devoted himself to this
duty with a fervid assiduity that has not often been ex-
ampled, and has never been surpassed. He went to work
with the zeal of a religious enthusiast, intent on purging
his church and his faith of the corruptions which lowered
it in the eyes of men. There was no part or order of
government so obscure, so remote, or so complex, as to
escape his acute and persevering observation.

Burke's object, in his schemes for Economical Reform,
was less to husband the public resources and relieve the
tax-payer—though this aim could not have been absent
from his mind, overburdened as England then was with
the charges of the American war — than to cut off the
channels which supplied the corruption of the House of
Commons. The full title of the first project which he
presented to the legislature (February, 1780), was A Plan
for the Better Security of the Independence of Parliament, and the Economical Reformation of the Civil and
other Establishments. It was to the former that he deemed the latter to be the most direct road. The strength
of the administration in the House was due to the gifts
which the Minister had in his hands to dispense. Men
voted with the side which could reward their fidelity. It
was the number of sinecure places and unpublished pensions which, along with the controllable influence of peers
and nabobs, furnished the Minister with an irresistible
lever: the avarice and the degraded public spirit of the
recipients supplied the required fulcrum. Burke knew
that in sweeping away these factitious places and secret
pensions, he would be robbing the Court of its chief im-

plements of corruption, and protecting the representative
against his chief motive in selling his country. He conceived that he would thus be promoting a far more infal-
lible means than any scheme of electoral reform could
have provided, for reviving the integrity and independence of the House of Commons. In his eyes, the evil
resided not in the constituencies, but in their representatives; not in the small number of the one, but in the
smaller integrity of the other.

The evil did not stop where it began. It was not merely that the sinister motive, thus engendered in the minds
of too lax and facile men, induced them to betray their
legislative trust, and barter their own uprightness and the
interests of the State. The acquisition of one of these nefarious bribes meant much more than a sinister vote. It
called into existence a champion of every inveterate abuse
that weighed on the resources of the country. There is a
well-known passage in the speech on Economical Reform,
in which the speaker shows what an insurmountable obstacle Lord Talbot had found in his attempt to carry out certain reforms in the royal household, in the fact that the
turnspit of the King's kitchen was a member of Parliament. "On that rock his whole adventure split — his
whole scheme of economy was dashed to pieces; his department became more expensive than ever; the Civil List
debt accumulated." Interference with the expenses of the
household meant interference with the perquisites or fees
of this legislative turnspit, and the rights of sinecures were
too sacred to be touched. In comparison with them, it
counted for nothing that the King's tradesmen went unpaid, and became bankrupt; that the judges were unpaid;
that " the justice of the kingdom bent and gave way; the
foreign ministers remained inactive and unprovided; the

system of Europe was dissolved; the chain of our alliances was broken; all the wheels of Government at home and abroad were stopped. *The king's turnspit was a member of Parliament.*[1] This office, and numbers of others exactly like it, existed solely because the House of Commons was crowded with venal men. The post of royal scullion meant a vote that could be relied upon under every circumstance and in all emergencies. And each incumbent of such an office felt his honour and interests concerned in the defence of all other offices of the same scandalous description. There was thus maintained a strong standing army of expensive, lax, and corrupting officials.

The royal household was a gigantic nest of costly jobbery and purposeless profusion. It retained all "the cumbrous charge of a Gothic establishment," though all its usage and accommodation had "shrunk into the polished littleness of modern elegance." The outlay was enormous. The expenditure on the court tables only was a thing unfathomable. Waste was the rule in every branch of it. There was an office for the Great Wardrobe, another office of the Robes, a third of the Groom of the Stole. For these three useless offices there were three useless treasurers. They all laid a heavy burden on the tax-payer, in order to supply a bribe to the member of Parliament. The plain remedy was to annihilate the subordinate treasuries. "Take away," was Burke's demand, "the whole establishment of detail in the household: the Treasurer, the Comptroller, the Cofferer of the Household, the Treasurer of the

[1] The Civil List at this time comprehended a great number of charges, such as those of which Burke speaks, that had nothing to do with the sovereign personally. They were slowly removed, the judicial and diplomatic charges being transferred on the accession of William IV.

5

Chamber, the Master of the Household, the whole Board
of Green Cloth; a vast number of subordinate offices in
the department of the Steward of the Household; the
whole establishment of the Great Wardrobe; the Removing Wardrobe; the Jewel Office; the Robes; the Board
of Works." The abolition of this confused and costly system would not only diminish expense and promote effi-
ciency; it would do still more excellent service in destroy-
ing the roots of parliamentary corruption. "Under other
governments a question of expense is only a question of
economy, and it is nothing more; with us, in every question of expense, there is always a mixture of constitutional
considerations."

Places and pensions, though the worst, were not by any
means the only stumbling-block in the way of pure and
well-ordered government. The administration of the estates of the Crown—the Principality, the Duchy of Corn-
wall, the Duchy of Lancaster, the County Palatine of Chester—was an elaborate system of obscure and unprofitable
expenditure. Wales had to herself eight judges, while no
more than twelve sufficed to perform the whole business
of justice in England, a country ten times as large, and a
hundred times as opulent. Wales, and each of the duch-
ies, had its own exchequer. Every one of these principali-
ties, said Burke, has the apparatus of a kingdom, for the
jurisdiction over a few private estates; it has the formality
and charge of the Exchequer of Great Britain, for collecting the rents of a country squire. They were the field, in
his expressive phrase, of mock jurisdictions and mimic rev-
enues, of difficult trifles and laborious fooleries. "It was
but the other day that that pert factious fellow, the Duke
of Lancaster, presumed to fly in the face of his liege lord,
our gracious sovereign—presumed to go to law with the

King. The object is neither your business nor mine. Which of the parties got the better I really forget. The material point is that the suit cost about 15,000*l*. But as the Duke of Lancaster is but agent of Duke Humphrey, and not worth a groat, our sovereign was obliged to pay the costs of both." The system which involved these costly absurdities, Burke proposed entirely to abolish. In the same spirit he wished to dispose of the Crown lands and the forest lands, which it was for the good of the community, not less than of the Crown itself, to throw into the hands of private owners.

One of the most important of these projected reforms, and one which its author did not flinch from carrying out two years later to his own loss, related to the office of Paymaster. This functionary was accustomed to hold large balances of the public money in his own hands and for his own profit, for long periods, owing to a complex system of accounts which was so rigorous as entirely to defeat its own object. The Paymaster could not, through the multiplicity of forms and the exaction of impossible conditions, get a prompt acquittance. The audit sometimes did not take place for years after the accounts were virtually closed. Meanwhile, the money accumulated in his hands, and its profits were his legitimate perquisite. The first Lord Holland, for example, held the balances of his office from 1765, when he retired, until 1778, when they were audited. During this time he realized, as the interest on the use of these balances, nearly two hundred and fifty thousand pounds. Burke diverted these enormous gains into the coffers of the state. He fixed the Paymaster's salary at four thousand pounds a year, and was himself the first person who accepted the curtailed income.

Not the most fervid or brilliant of Burke's pieces, yet

the Speech on Economical Reform is certainly not the least
instructive or impressive of them.   It gives a suggestive
view of the relations existing at that time between the
House of Commons and the Court.   It reveals the narrow
and unpatriotic spirit of the King and the ministers, who
could resist proposals so reasonable in themselves, and so
remedial in their effects, at a time when the nation was
suffering the heavy and distressing burdens of the most
disastrous war that our country has ever carried on.   It
is especially interesting as an illustration of its author's
political capacity.   At a moment when committees, and
petitions, and great county meetings showed how thoroughly the national anger was roused against the existing
system, Burke came to the front of affairs with a scheme,
of which the most striking characteristic proved to be that
it was profoundly temperate.   Bent on the extirpation of
the system, he had no ill-will towards the men who had
happened to flourish in it.   "I never will suffer," he said,
"any man or description of men to suffer from errors that
naturally have grown out of the abusive constitution of
those offices which I propose to regulate.   If I cannot reform with equity, I will not reform at all."   Exasperated
as he was by the fruitlessness of his opposition to a policy
which he detested from the bottom of his soul, it would
have been little wonderful if he had resorted to every
weapon of his unrivalled rhetorical armoury, in order to
discredit and overthrow the whole scheme of government.
Yet nothing could have been further from his mind than
any violent or extreme idea of this sort.   Many years afterwards he took credit to himself less for what he did on
this occasion, than for what he prevented from being done.
People were ready for a new modelling of the two Houses
of Parliament, as well as for grave modifications of the

Prerogative. Burke resisted this temper unflinchingly. "I had," he says, "a state to preserve, as well as a state to reform. I had a people to gratify, but not to inflame or to mislead." He then recounts without exaggeration the pains and caution with which he sought reform, while steering clear of innovation. He heaved the lead every inch of way he made. It is grievous to think that a man who could assume such an attitude at such a time, who could give this kind of proof of his skill in the great, the difficult, art of governing, only held a fifth-rate office for some time less than a twelvemonth.

The year of the project of Economic Reform (1780) is usually taken as the date when Burke's influence and repute were at their height. He had not been tried in the fire of official responsibility, and his impetuosity was still under a degree of control which not long afterwards was fatally weakened by an over-mastering irritability of constitution. High as his character was now in the ascendant, it was in the same year that Burke suffered the sharp mortification of losing his seat at Bristol. His speech before the election is one of the best known of all his performances; and it well deserves to be so, for it is surpassed by none in gravity, elevation, and moral dignity. We can only wonder that a constituency which could suffer itself to be addressed on this high level should have allowed the small selfishness of local interest to weigh against such wisdom and nobility. But Burke soon found in the course of his canvas that he had no chance, and he declined to go to the poll. On the previous day one of his competitors had fallen down dead. "*What shadows we are,*" said Burke, "*and what shadows we pursue!*"

In 1782 Lord North's government came to an end, and the King "was pleased," as Lord North quoted with jest-

ing irony from the Gazette, to send for Lord Rockingham,
Charles Fox, and Lord Shelburne. Members could hardly
believe their own eyes, as they saw Lord North and the
members of a government which had been in place for
twelve years, now lounging on the opposition benches in
their great-coats, frocks, and boots, while Fox and Burke
shone in the full dress that was then worn by ministers,
and cut unwonted figures with swords, lace, and hair pow-
der. Sheridan was made an under-secretary of state, and
to the younger Pitt was offered his choice of various minor posts, which he haughtily refused. Burke, to whom
on their own admission the party owed everything, was
appointed Paymaster of the Forces, with a salary of four
thousand pounds a year. His brother, Richard Burke,
was made Secretary of the Treasury. His son, Richard,
was named to be his father's deputy at the Pay Office,
with a salary of five hundred pounds a year.

This singular exclusion from cabinet office of the most
powerful genius of the party has naturally given rise to
abundant criticism ever since. It will be convenient to
say what there is to be said on this subject, in connexion
with the events of 1788 (below, p. 136), because there hap-
pens to exist some useful information about the ministerial crisis of that year, which sheds a clearer light upon the
arrangements of six years before. Meanwhile it is enough
to say that Burke himself had most reasonably looked to
some higher post. There is the distinct note of the hu-
mility of mortified pride in a letter written in reply to
some one who had applied to him for a place. "You
have been misinformed," he says; "I make no part of
the ministerial arrangement. Something in the official
line may possibly be thought fit for my measure." Burke
knew that his position in the country entitled him to

something above the official line. In a later year, when
he felt himself called upon to defend his pension, he described what his position was in the momentous crisis from
1780 to 1782, and Burke's habitual veraciousness forbids
us to treat the description as in any way exaggerated.
" By what accident it matters not," he says, " nor upon
what desert, but just then, and in the midst of that hunt
of obloquy which has ever pursued me with a full cry
through life, I had obtained a very full degree of public
confidence. . . . Nothing to prevent disorder was omitted;
when it appeared, nothing to subdue it was left uncoun-
selled nor unexecuted, as far as I could prevail. At the
time I speak of, and having a momentary lead, so aided
and so encouraged, and as a feeble instrument in a mighty
hand—I do not say I saved my country—I am sure I did
my country important service. There were few indeed
that did not at that time acknowledge it—and that time
was thirteen years ago. It was but one view, that no man
in the kingdom better deserved an honourable provision
should be made for him."[1]

We have seen that Burke had fixed the Paymaster's
salary at four thousand pounds, and had destroyed the extravagant perquisites. The other economical reforms which
were actually effected fell short by a long way of those
which Burke had so industriously devised and so forcibly
recommended. In 1782, while Burke declined to spare
his own office, the chief of the cabinet conferred upon
Barré a pension of over three thousand a year; above ten
times the amount, as has been said, which, in Lord Rockingham's own judgment, as expressed in the new Bill,
ought henceforth to be granted to any one person whatever. This shortcoming, however, does not detract from

[1] *Letter to a Noble Lord.*

Burke's merit. He was not responsible for it. The eloquence, ingenuity, diligence, above all, the sagacity and the
justice of this great effort of 1780, are none the less worthy of our admiration and regard because, in 1782, his
chiefs, partly perhaps out of a newborn deference for the
feelings of their royal master, showed that the possession
of office had sensibly cooled the ardent aspirations proper
to Opposition.

The events of the twenty months between the resignation of Lord North (1782) and the accession of Pitt to the
office of Prime Minister (December, 1783) mark an important crisis in political history, and they mark an important crisis in Burke's career and hopes. Lord Rockingham had just been three months in office when he died
(July, 1782). This dissolved the bond that held the two
sections of the ministry together, and let loose a flood of
rival ambitions and sharp animosities. Lord Shelburne
believed himself to have an irresistible claim to the chief
post in the administration; among other reasons, because
he might have had it before Lord Rockingham three
months earlier, if he had so chosen. The King supported
him, not from any partiality to his person, but because he
dreaded and hated Charles Fox. The character of Shelburne is one of the perplexities of the time. His views on
peace and free trade make him one of the precursors of
the Manchester School. No minister was so well informed as to the threads of policy in foreign countries. He
was the intimate or the patron of men who now stand out
as among the first lights of that time — of Morellet, of
Priestley, of Bentham. Yet a few months of power seem
to have disclosed faults of character which left him without a single political friend, and blighted him with irrepa-
rable discredit. Fox, who was now the head of the Rock-

ingham section of the Whigs, had, before the death of the
late premier, been on the point of refusing to serve any
longer with Lord Shelburne, and he now very promptly
refused to serve under him. When Parliament met after
Rockingham's death, gossips noticed that Fox and Burke
continued, long after the Speaker had taken the chair, to
walk backwards and forwards in the Court of Requests,
engaged in earnest conversation. According to one story,
Burke was very reluctant to abandon an office whose emoluments were as convenient to him as to his spendthrift
colleague. According to another and more probable legend, it was Burke who hurried the rupture, and stimulated Fox's jealousy of Shelburne. The Duke of Richmond
disapproved of the secession, and remained in the government. Sheridan also disapproved, but he sacrificed his
personal conviction to loyalty to Fox.

If Burke was responsible for the break-up of the government, then he was the instigator of a blunder that must
be pronounced not only disastrous but culpable. It lowered the legitimate spirit of party to the nameless spirit of
faction. The dangers from which the old liberties of the
realm had just emerged have been described by no one so
forcibly as by Burke himself. No one was so convinced
as Burke that the only way of withstanding the arbitrary
and corrupting policy of the Court was to form a strong
Whig party. No one knew better than he the sovereign
importance and the immense difficulty of repairing the
ruin of the last twelve years by a good peace. The Rockingham or Foxite section were obviously unable to form
an effective party with serious expectation of power, unless they had allies. They might, no doubt, from personal dislike to Lord Shelburne, refuse to work under him;
but personal dislike could be no excuse for formally and
    5*

violently working against him, when his policy was their
own, and when its success was recognized by them no less
than by him as of urgent moment.   Instead of either
working with the other section of their party, or of supporting from below the gangway that which was the policy of both sections, they sought to return to power by
coalescing with the very man whose criminal subservience
to the King's will had brought about the catastrophe that
Shelburne was repairing.   Burke must share the blame of
this famous transaction.   He was one of the most furious
assailants of the new ministry.   He poured out a fresh invective against Lord Shelburne every day.   Cynical contemporaries laughed as they saw him in search of more
and more humiliating parallels, ransacking all literature
from the Bible and the Roman history down to Mother
Goose's tales.   His passion carried him so far as to breed
a reaction in those who listened to him. " I think," wrote
Mason from Yorkshire, where Burke had been on a visit
to Lord Fitzwilliam in the autumn of 1782, "that Burke's
mad obloquy against Lord Shelburne, and these insolent
pamphlets in which he must have had a hand, will do
more to fix him (Shelburne) in his office than anything
else."

This result would have actually followed, for the nation
was ill pleased at the immoral alliance between the Fox-
ites and the man whom, if they had been true to their
opinions a thousand times repeated, they ought at that
moment to have been impeaching.   The Dissenters, who
had hitherto been his enthusiastic admirers, but who are
rigid above other men in their demand of political consistency, lamented Burke's fall in joining the Coalition, as
Priestley told him many years after, as the fall of a friend
and a brother.   But Shelburne threw away the game.

"His falsehoods," says Horace Walpole, "his flatteries, duplicity, insincerity, arrogance, contradictions, neglect of his friends, with all the kindred of all these faults, were the daily topics of contempt and ridicule; and his folly shut his eyes, nor did he perceive that so very rapid a fall must have been owing to his own incapacity." This is the testimony of a hostile witness. It is borne out, however, by a circumstance of striking significance. When the King recovered the reins at the end of 1783, not only did he send for Pitt instead of for Shelburne, but Pitt himself neither invited Shelburne to join him, nor in any way ever consulted him then or afterwards, though he had been Chancellor of the Exchequer in Shelburne's own administration.

Whatever the causes may have been, the administration fell in the spring of 1783. It was succeeded by the memorable ministry of the Coalition, in which Fox and Lord North divided the real power under the nominal lead of the Duke of Portland. Members saw Lord North squeezed up on the Treasury bench between two men who had a year before been daily menacing him with the axe and the block; and it was not North whom they blamed, but Burke and Fox. Burke had returned to the Pay Office. His first act there was unfortunate. He restored to their position two clerks who had been suspended for malversation, and against whom proceedings were then pending. When attacked for this in the House, he showed an irritation which would have carried him to gross lengths, if Fox and Sheridan had not by main force pulled him down into his seat by the tails of his coat. The restoration of the clerks was an indefensible error of judgment, and its indiscretion was heightened by the kind of defence which Burke tried to set up. When we wonder at Burke's exclusion from great offices, this case of Powell and Bembridge should not be forgotten.

The decisive event in the history of the Coalition Government was the India Bill. The Reports of the various select committees upon Indian affairs—the most important of them all, the ninth and eleventh, having been drawn up by Burke himself—had shown conclusively that the existing system of government was thoroughly corrupt and thoroughly inadequate. It is ascertained pretty conclusively that the bill for replacing that system was conceived and drawn by Burke, and that to him belongs whatever merit or demerit it might possess. It was Burke who infected Fox with his own ardour, and then, as Moore justly says, the self-kindling power of Fox's eloquence threw such fire into his defence of the measure, that he forgot, and his hearers never found out, that his views were not originally and spontaneously his own. The novelty on which the great stress of discussion was laid, was that the bill withdrew power from the Board of Directors, and vested the government for four years in a commission of seven persons named in the bill, and not removable by the House.

Burke was so convinced of the incurable iniquity of the Company, so persuaded that it was not only full of abuses, but, as he said, one of the most corrupt and destructive tyrannies that probably ever existed in the world, as to be content with nothing short of the absolute deprivation of its power. He avowed himself no lover of names, and that he only contended for good government, from whatever quarter it might come. But the idea of good government coming from the Company he declared to be desperate and untenable. This intense animosity, which, considering his long and close familiarity with the infamies of the rule of the Company's servants, was not un-

natural, must be allowed, however, to have blinded him to
the grave objections which really existed to his scheme.
In the first place, the Bill was indisputably inconsistent
with the spirit of his revered Constitution.   For the legislature to assume the power of naming the members of an
executive body, was an extraordinary and mischievous innovation.   Then, to put patronage, which has been estimated by a sober authority at about three hundred thousand pounds a year, into the hands of the House of Commons, was still more mischievous and still less justifiable.
Worst of all, from the point of view of the projectors
themselves, after a certain time the nomination of the
Commissioners would fall to the Crown, and this might in
certain contingencies increase to a most dangerous extent
the ascendancy of the royal authority.   If Burke's measure
had been carried, moreover, the patronage would have been
transferred to a body much less competent than the Directors to judge of the qualities required in the fulfilment of this
or that administrative charge.   Indian promotion would
have followed parliamentary and party interest.   In the
hands of the Directors there was at least a partial security,
in their professional knowledge, and their personal interest
in the success of their government, that places would not
be given away on irrelevant considerations.   Their system,
with all its faults, insured the acquisition of a certain considerable competency in administration, before a servant
reached an elevation at which he could do much harm.

Burke defended the bill (December 1, 1783) in one of
the speeches which rank only below his greatest, and it
contains two or three passages of unsurpassed energy and
impressiveness.   Everybody knows the fine page about
Fox as the descendant of Henry IV. of France, and the
happy quotation from Silius Italicus.   Every book of Brit-

ish eloquence contains the magnificent description of the young magistrates who undertake the government and the spoliation of India; how, "animated with all the avarice of age and all the impetuosity of youth, they roll in one after another, wave after wave; and there is nothing before the eyes of the natives but an endless, hopeless prospect of new flights of birds of prey and of passage, with appetites continually renewing for a food that is continually wasting." How they return home laden with spoil; "their prey is lodged in England; and the cries of India are given to seas and winds, to be blown about, in every breaking up of the monsoon, over a remote and unhearing ocean." How in India all the vices operate by which sudden fortune is acquired; while in England are often displayed by the same person the virtues which dispense hereditary wealth, so that "here the manufacturer and the husbandman will bless the just and punctual hand that in India has torn the cloth from the loom, or wrested the scanty portion of rice and salt from the peasant of Bengal, or wrung from him the very opium in which he forgot his oppression and his oppressors."

No degree of eloquence, however, could avail to repair faults alike in structure and in tactics. The whole design was a masterpiece of hardihood, miscalculation, and mismanagement. The combination of interests against the bill was instant, and it was indeed formidable. The great army of returned nabobs, of directors, of proprietors of East India stock, rose up in all its immense force. Every member of every corporation that enjoyed privilege by charter felt the attack on the Company as if it had been a blow directed against himself. The general public had no particular passion for purity or good government, and the best portion of the public was disgusted with the

Coalition. The King saw his chance. With politic audacity he put so strong a personal pressure on the peers, that they threw out the Bill (December, 1783). It was to no purpose that Fox compared the lords to the Janissaries of a Turkish Sultan, and the King's letter to Temple to the rescript in which Tiberius ordered the upright Sejanus to be destroyed. Ministers were dismissed, the young Pitt was installed in their place, and the Whigs were ruined. As a party, they had a few months of office after Pitt's death, but they were excluded from power for half a century.

CHAPTER VI.

BURKE AND HIS FRIENDS.

THOUGH Burke had, at a critical period of his life, definitely abandoned the career of letters, he never withdrew from close intimacy with the groups who still live for us in the pages of Boswell, as no other literary group in our history lives. Goldsmith's famous lines in *Retaliation* show how they all deplored that he should to party give up what was meant for mankind. They often told one another that Edmund Burke was the man whose genius pointed him out as the triumphant champion of faith and sound philosophy against deism, atheism, and David Hume. They loved to see him, as Goldsmith said, wind into his subject like a serpent. Everybody felt at the Literary Club that he had no superior in knowledge, and in colloquial dialectics only one equal. Garrick was there, and of all the names of the time he is the man whom one would perhaps most willingly have seen, because the gifts which threw not only Englishmen, but Frenchmen like Diderot, and Germans like Lichtenberg, into amazement and ecstasy, are exactly those gifts which literary description can do least to reproduce. Burke was one of his strongest admirers, and there was no more zealous attendant at the closing series of performances in which the great monarch of the stage abdicated his throne. In the last pages that he wrote, Burke refers to his ever dear

friend Garrick, dead nearly twenty years before, as the first
of actors, because he was the acutest observer of nature
that he had ever known.

Among men who pass for being more serious than
players, Robertson was often in London society, and he
attracted Burke by his largeness and breadth. He sent
a copy of his history of America, and Burke thanked
him with many stately compliments for having employed
philosophy to judge of manners, and from manners having drawn new resources of philosophy. Gibbon was
there, but the bystanders felt what was too crudely expressed by Mackintosh, that Gibbon might have been taken
from a corner of Burke's mind without ever being missed.
Though Burke and Gibbon constantly met, it is not likely that, until the Revolution, there was much intimacy between them, in spite of the respect which each of them
might well have had for the vast knowledge of the other.
When the *Decline and Fall* was published, Burke read it
as everybody else did; but he told Reynolds that he disliked the style, as very affected, mere frippery and tinsel.
Sir Joshua himself was neither a man of letters nor a keen
politician; but he was full of literary ideas and interests,
and he was among Burke's warmest and most constant
friends, following him with an admiration and reverence
that even Johnson sometimes thought excessive. The
reader of Reynolds's famous Discourses will probably share
the wonder of his contemporaries, that a man whose time
was so absorbed in the practice of his art should have
proved himself so excellent a master in the expression of
some of its principles. Burke was commonly credited
with a large share in their composition, but the evidence
goes no further than that Reynolds used to talk them over
with him. The friendship between the pair was full and

unalloyed. What Burke admired in the great artist was his sense and his morals, no less than his genius; and to a man of his fervid and excitable temper there was the most attractive of all charms in Sir Joshua's placidity, gentleness, evenness, and the habit, as one of his friends described it, of being the same all the year round. When Reynolds died in 1792, he appointed Burke one of his executors, and left him a legacy of two thousand pounds, besides cancelling a bond of the same amount.

Johnson, however, is the only member of that illustrious company who can profitably be compared with Burke in strength and impressiveness of personality, in a large sensibility at once serious and genial, in brooding care for all the fulness of human life. This striking pair were the two complements of a single noble and solid type, holding tenaciously, in a century of dissolvent speculation, to the best ideas of a society that was slowly passing. They were powerless to hinder the inevitable transformation. One of them did not even dimly foresee it. But both of them help us to understand how manliness and reverence, strength and tenderness, love of truth and pity for man, all flourished under old institutions and old ways of thinking, into which the forces of the time were even then silently breathing a new spirit. The friendship between Burke and Johnson lasted as long as they lived; and if we remember that Johnson was a strong Tory, and declared that the first Whig was the devil, and habitually talked about cursed Whigs and bottomless Whigs, it is an extraordinary fact that his relations with the greatest Whig writer and politician of his day were marked by a cordiality, respect, and admiration that never varied nor wavered. "Burke," he said in a well-known passage, "is such a man that if you met him for the first time in the street, where you were stopped by a drove of oxen, and you and he stepped aside to take shelter but for five minutes, he'd talk to you in such a manner that, when you parted, you would say, This is an extraordinary man. He is never what we would call humdrum; never unwilling to begin to talk, nor in haste to leave off." That Burke was as good a listener as he was a talker, Johnson never would allow. "So desirous is he to talk," he said, "that if one is talking at this end of the table, he'll talk to somebody at the other end." Johnson was far too good a critic, and too honest a man, to assent to a remark of Robertson's, that Burke had wit. "No, sir," said the sage, most truly, "he never succeeds there. 'Tis low, 'tis conceit." Wit apart, he described Burke as the only man whose common conversation corresponded to his general fame in the world; take up whatever topic you might please, he was ready to meet you. When Burke found a seat in Parliament, Johnson said, "Now we who know Burke, know that he will be one of the first men in the country." He did not grudge that Burke should be the first man in the House of Commons, for Burke, he said, was always the first man everywhere. Once when he was ill, somebody mentioned Burke's name. Johnson cried out, "That fellow calls forth all my powers; were I to see Burke now it would kill me."

Burke heartily returned this high appreciation. When some flatterer hinted that Johnson had taken more than his right share of the evening's talk, Burke said, "Nay, it is enough for me to have rung the bell for him." Some one else spoke of a successful imitation of Johnson's style. Burke with vehemence denied the success: the performance, he said, had the pomp, but not the force of the original; the nodosities of the oak, but not its strength; the

contortions of the sibyl, but none of the inspiration.
When Burke showed the old sage of Bolt Court over his
fine house and pleasant gardens at Beaconsfield, *Non in-
video equidem*, Johnson said, with placid good-will, *miror
magis*. They always parted in the deep and pregnant
phrase of a sage of our own day, *except in opinion not dis-
agreeing*. In truth, the explanation of the sympathy between them is not far to seek. We may well believe that
Johnson was tacitly alive to the essentially conservative
spirit of Burke even in his most Whiggish days. And
Burke penetrated the liberality of mind in a Tory, who
called out with loud indignation that the Irish were in a
most unnatural state, for there the minority prevailed over
the majority, and the severity of the persecution exercised by
the Protestants of Ireland against the Catholics, exceeded
that of the ten historic persecutions of the Christian Church.

The parties at Beaconsfield, and the evenings at the
Turk's Head in Gerard Street, were contemporary with the
famous days at Holbach's country house at Grandval.
When we think of the reckless themes that were so recklessly discussed by Holbach, Diderot, and the rest of that
indefatigable band, we feel that, as against the French
philosophic party, an English Tory like Johnson and an
English Whig like Burke would have found their own
differences too minute to be worth considering. If the
group from the Turk's Head could have been transported
for an afternoon to Grandval, perhaps Johnson would have
been the less impatient and disgusted of the two. He had
the capacity of the more genial sort of casuist for playing
with subjects, even moral subjects, with the freedom, versatility, and ease that are proper to literature. Burke, on
the contrary, would not have failed to see, as indeed we
know that he did not fail to see, that a social pandemo-

nium was being prepared in this intellectual paradise of
open questions, where God and a future life, marriage and
the family, every dogma of religion, every prescription of
morality, and all those mysteries and pieties of human life
which have been sanctified by the reverence of ages, were
being busily pulled to pieces, as if they had been toys in
the hands of a company of sportive children.   Even the
Beggar's Opera Burke could not endure to hear praised
for its wit or its music, because his mind was filled by
thought of its misplaced levity, and he only saw the mischief which such a performance tended to do to society.
It would be hard to defend his judgment in this particular
case, but it serves to show how Burke was never content
with the literary point of view, and how ready and vigilant
he was for effects more profound than those of formal
criticism.   It is true that Johnson was sometimes not less
austere in condemning a great work of art for its bad
morality.   The only time when he was really angry with
Hannah More was on his finding that she had read *Tom
Jones*—that vicious book, he called it; he hardly knew a
more corrupt work.   Burke's tendency towards severity
of moral judgment, however, never impaired the geniality
and tenderness of his relations with those whom he loved.
Bennet Langton gave Boswell an affecting account of
Burke's last interview with Johnson.   A few days before
the old man's death, Burke and four or five other friends
were sitting round his bedside.   "Mr. Burke said to him,
'I am afraid, sir, such a number of us may be oppressive
to you.'   'No, sir,' said Johnson, 'it is not so; and I must
be in a wretched state, indeed, when your company is not
a delight to me.'   Mr. Burke, in a tremulous voice, expressive of being very tenderly affected, replied, 'My dear sir,
you have always been too good to me.'   Immediately af-

terwards he went away. This was the last circumstance
in the acquaintance of these two eminent men."

One of Burke's strongest political intimacies was only
less interesting and significant than his friendship with
Johnson. William Dowdeswell had been Chancellor of
the Exchequer in the short Rockingham administration of
1765. He had no brilliant gifts, but he had what was
then thought a profound knowledge both of the principles
and details of the administration of the national revenue.
He was industrious, steadfast, clear-headed, inexorably upright. "Immersed in the greatest affairs," as Burke said
in his epitaph, "he never lost the ancient, native, genuine,
English character of a country gentleman." And this
was the character in which Burke now and always saw
not only the true political barrier against despotism on
the one hand and the rabble on the other, but the best
moral type of civic virtue. Those who admire Burke, but
cannot share his admiration for the country gentleman,
will perhaps justify him by the assumption that he clothed
his favourite with ideal qualities which ought, even if they
did not, to have belonged to that position.

In his own modest imitation and in his own humble
scale, he was a pattern of the activity in public duty, the
hospitality towards friends, the assiduous protection of
neglected worth, which ought to be among the chief virtues of high station. It would perhaps be doubly unsafe
to take for granted that many of our readers have both
turned over the pages of Crabbe's *Borough*, and carried
away in their minds from that moderately affecting poem,
the description of Eusebius—

> That pious moralist, that reasoning saint !
> Can I of worth like thine, Eusebius, speak ?
> The man is willing, but the muse is weak.

Eusebius is intended for Burke, and the portrait is a literary tribute for more substantial services. When Crabbe
came up from his native Aldborough, with three pounds
and a case of surgical instruments in his trunk, he fondly
believed that a great patron would be found to watch over
his transformation from an unsuccessful apothecary into a
popular poet. He wrote to Lord North and Lord Shelburne, but they did not answer his letters; booksellers returned his copious manuscripts; the three pounds gradually disappeared; the surgical instruments went to the
pawnbroker's; and the poet found himself an outcast on
the world, without a friend, without employment, and
without bread. He owed money for his lodging, and was
on the very eve of being sent to prison, when it occurred
to him to write to Burke. It was the moment (1781)
when the final struggle with Lord North was at its fiercest,
and Burke might have been absolved if, in the stress of
conflict, he had neglected a begging-letter. As it was, the
manliness and simplicity of Crabbe's application touched
him. He immediately made an appointment with the
young poet, and convinced himself of his worth. He not
only relieved Crabbe's immediate distress with a sum of
money that, as we know, came from no affluence of his
own, but carried him off to Beaconsfield, installed him
there as a member of the family, and took as much pains
to find a printer for *The Library* and *The Village*, as if
they had been his own poems. In time he persuaded the
Bishop of Norwich to admit Crabbe, in spite of his want
of a regular qualification, to holy orders. He then commended him to the notice of Lord Chancellor Thurlow.
Crabbe found the Tiger less formidable than his terrifying
reputation, for Thurlow at their first interview presented
him with a hundred-pound note, and afterwards gave him

a living. The living was of no great value, it is true; and
it was Burke who, with untiring friendship, succeeded in
procuring something like a substantial position for him, by
inducing the Duke of Rutland to make the young parson
his chaplain. Henceforth Crabbe's career was assured, and
he never forgot to revere and bless the man to whose generous hand he owed his deliverance.

Another of Burke's clients, of whom we hardly know
whether to say that he is more or less known to our age
than Crabbe, is Barry, a painter of disputable eminence.
The son of a seafarer at Cork, he had been introduced to
Burke in Dublin in 1762, was brought over to England by
him, introduced to some kind of employment, and finally
sent, with funds provided by the Burkes, to study art on
the Continent. It was characteristic of Burke's willingness not only to supply money, but, what is a far rarer
form of kindness, to take active trouble, that he should
have followed the raw student with long and careful letters of advice upon the proper direction of his studies.
For five years Barry was maintained abroad by the Burkes.
Most unhappily for himself, he was cursed with an irritable
and perverse temper, and he lacked even the elementary
arts of conduct. Burke was generous to the end, with
that difficult and uncommon kind of generosity which
moves independently of gratitude or ingratitude in the
receiver.

From his earliest days Burke had been the eager friend
of people in distress. While he was still a student at the
Temple, or a writer for the booksellers, he picked up a
curious creature in the park, in such unpromising circumstances that he could not forbear to take him under his
instant protection. This was Joseph Emin, the Armenian,
who had come to Europe from India with strange heroic

ideas in his head as to the deliverance of his countrymen.
Burke instantly urged him to accept the few shillings that
he happened to have in his purse, and seems to have found
employment for him as a copyist, until fortune brought
other openings to the singular adventurer.   For foreign
visitors Burke had always a singular considerateness.
Two Brahmins came to England as agents of Ragonaut
Rao, and at first underwent intolerable things rather from
the ignorance than the unkindness of our countrymen.
Burke no sooner found out what was passing, than he carried them down to Beaconsfield, and as it was summer-
time he gave them for their separate use a spacious gar-
den-house, where they were free to prepare their food and
perform the rites as their religion prescribed.   Nothing
was so certain to command his fervid sympathy as strict
adherence to the rules and ceremonies of an ancient and
sacred ordering.

If he never failed to perform the offices to which we
are bound by the common sympathy of men, it is satis-
factory to think that Burke in return received a measure
of these friendly services.   Among those who loved him
best was Doctor Brocklesby, the tender physician who
watched and soothed the last hours of Johnson.   When we
remember how Burke's soul was harassed by private cares,
chagrined by the untoward course of public events, and
mortified by neglect from friends no less than by virulent
reproach from foes, it makes us feel very kindly towards
Brocklesby, to read what he wrote to Burke in 1788 :

My very dear friend,—

    My veneration of your public conduct for many years past, and
my real affection for your private virtues and transcendent worth,
made me yesterday take a liberty with you in a moment's conversation at my house, to make you an instant present of 1000*l.*, which for

years past I had by will destined as a testimony of my regard on my decease. This you modestly desired me not to think of; but I told you what I now repeat, that unfavoured as I have lived for a long life, unnoticed professionally by any party of men, and though unknown at court, I am rich enough to spare to virtue (what others waste in vice) the above sum, and still reserve an annual income greater than I spend. I shall receive at the India House a bill I have discounted for 1000*l.* on the 4th of next month, and then shall be happy that you will accept this proof of my sincere love and es-teem, and let me add, *Si res ampla domi similisque affectibus esset,* I should be happy to repeat the like every year."

The mere transcription of the friendly man's good letter has something of the effect of an exercise of religion. And it was only one of a series of kind acts on the part of the same generous giver.

It is always interesting in the case of a great man to know how he affected the women of his acquaintance. Women do not usually judge character either so kindly or so soundly as men do, for they lack that knowledge of the ordeals of practical life, which gives both justice and char-ity to such verdicts. But they are more susceptible than most men are to devotion and nobility in character. The little group of the blue-stockings of the day regarded the great master of knowledge and eloquence with mixed feel-ings. They felt for Burke the adoring reverence which women offer, with too indiscriminate a trust, to men of commanding power. In his case it was the moral lofti-ness of his character that inspired them, as much as the splendour of his ability. Of Sheridan or of Fox they could not bear to hear; of Burke they could not hear enough. Hannah More, and Mrs. Elizabeth Carter, the learned translator of Epictetus, and Fanny Burney, the au-thor of *Evelina* and *Cecilia,* were all proud of his notice, even while they glowed with anger at his sympathy with

American rebels, his unkind words about the King, and his
cruel persecution of poor Mr. Hastings. It was at Mrs.
Vesey's evening parties, given on the Tuesdays on which
the Club dined at the Turk's Head, that he often had long
chats with Hannah More. She had to forget what she
called his political malefactions, before she could allow herself to admire his high spirits and good-humour. This
was after the events of the Coalition, and her Memoirs,
like the change in the mind of the Dissenters towards
Burke, show what a fall that act of faction was believed
to mark in his character. When he was rejected for Bristol, she moralized on the catastrophe by the quaint reflection that Providence has wisely contrived to render all its
dispensations equal, by making those talents which set one
man so much above another of no esteem in the opinion
of those who are without them.

Miss Burney has described her flutter of spirits when
she first found herself in company with Burke (1782). It
was at Sir Joshua's house on the top of Richmond Hill,
and she tells, with her usual effusion, how she was impressed by Burke's noble figure and commanding air, his
penetrating and sonorous voice, his eloquent and copious
language, the infinite variety and rapidity of his discourse.
Burke had something to say on every subject, from bits
of personal gossip, up to the sweet and melting landscape
that lay in all its beauty before their windows on the ter-
race. He was playful, serious, fantastic, wise. When they
next met, the great man completed his conquest by expressing his admiration of *Evelina*. Gibbon assured her
that he had read the whole five volumes in a day; but
Burke declared the feat was impossible, for he had himself
read it through without interruption, and it had cost him
three days. He showed his regard for the authoress in a

more substantial way than by compliments and criticism. His last act, before going out of office, in 1783, was to procure for Dr. Burney the appointment of organist at the chapel of Chelsea.

We have spoken of the dislike of these excellent women for Sheridan and Fox. In Sheridan's case Burke did not much disagree with them. Their characters were as unlike and as antipathetic as those of two men could be; and to antipathy of temperament was probably added a kind of rivalry, which may justly have affected one of them with an irritated humiliation. Sheridan was twenty years younger than Burke, and did not come into Parliament until Burke had fought the prolonged battle of the American war, and had achieved the victory of Economic Reform. Yet Sheridan was immediately taken up by the party, and became the intimate and counsellor of Charles Fox, its leader, and of the Prince of Wales, its patron. That Burke never failed to do full justice to Sheridan's brilliant genius, or to bestow generous and unaffected praise on his oratorical successes, there is ample evidence. He was of far too high and veracious a nature to be capable of the disparaging tricks of a poor jealousy. The humiliation lay in the fact that circumstances had placed Sheridan in a position which made it natural for the world to measure them with one another. Burke could no more like Sheridan than he could like the *Beggar's Opera.* Sheridan had a levity, a want of depth, a laxity, and dispersion of feeling, to which no degree of intellectual brilliancy could reconcile a man of such profound moral energy and social conviction as Burke.

The thought will perhaps occur to the reader that Fox was not less lax than Sheridan, and yet for Fox Burke long had the sincerest friendship. He was dissolute, in-

dolent, irregular, and the most insensate gambler that ever
squandered fortune after fortune over the faro-table. It
was his vices as much as his politics, that made George
III. hate Fox as an English Catiline. How came Burke
to accept a man of this character, first for his disciple,
then for his friend, and next for his leader? The answer
is a simple one. In spite of the disorders of his life, Fox,
from the time when his acquaintance with Burke began,
down to the time when it came to such disastrous end,
and for long years afterwards, was to the bottom of his
heart as passionate for freedom, justice, and beneficence as
Burke ever was. These great ends were as real, as constant, as overmastering in Fox as they were in Burke.
No man was ever more deeply imbued with the generous
impulses of great statesmanship, with chivalrous courage,
with the magnificent spirit of devotion to high imposing
causes. These qualities, we may be sure, and not his power as a debater and as a declaimer, won for him in Burke's
heart the admiration which found such splendid expression in a passage, that will remain as a stock piece of declamation for long generations after it was first poured out
as a sincere tribute of reverence and affection. Precisians,
like Lafayette, might choose to see their patriotic hopes
ruined rather than have them saved by Mirabeau, because
Mirabeau was a debauchee. Burke's public morality was
of stouter stuff, and he loved Fox because he knew that
under the stains and blemishes that had been left by a
deplorable education was that sterling, inexhaustible ore
in which noble sympathies are subtly compounded with
resplendent powers.

If he was warmly attached to his political friends,
Burke, at least before the Revolution, was usually on fair
terms in private life with his political opponents. There

were few men whose policy he disliked more than he disliked the policy of George Grenville. And we have seen
that he criticized Grenville in a pamphlet which did not
spare him. Yet Grenville and he did not refuse one another's hospitality, and were on the best terms to the very
end. Wilberforce, again, was one of the staunchest friends
of Pitt, and fought one of the greatest electioneering bat-
tles on Pitt's side in the struggle of 1784; but it made
no difference in Burke's relations with him. In 1787 a
coldness arose between them. Burke had delivered a
strong invective against the French Treaty. Wilberforce
said, "We can make allowance for the honourable gentleman, because we remember him in better days." The
retort greatly nettled Burke, but the feeling soon passed
away, and they both found a special satisfaction in the
dinner to which Wilberforce invited Burke every session.
"He was a great man," says Wilberforce. "I could never understand how at one time he grew to be so entirely
neglected."

Outside of both political and literary circles, among
Burke's correspondents was that wise and honest traveller
whose name is as inseparably bound up with the preparation of the French Revolution, as Burke's is bound up
with its sanguinary climax and fulfilment. Arthur Young,
by his Farmer's Letters, and Farmer's Calendar, and his
account of his travels in the southern counties of England
and elsewhere—the story of the more famous travels in
France was not published until 1792—had won a reputation as the best-informed agriculturist of his day. Within a year of his settlement at Beaconsfield, we find Burke
writing to consult Young on the mysteries of his new occupation. The reader may smile as he recognizes the
ardour, the earnestness, the fervid gravity of the political

speeches, in letters which discuss the merits of carrots in fattening porkers, and the precise degree to which they should be boiled. Burke throws himself just as eagerly into white peas and Indian corn, into cabbages that grow into head and cabbages that shoot into leaves, into experiments with pumpkin seed and wild parsnip, as if they had been details of the Stamp Act, or justice to Ireland. When he complains that it is scarcely possible for him, with his numerous avocations, to get his servants to enter fully into his views as to the right treatment of his crops, we can easily understand that his farming did not help him to make money. It is impossible that he should have had time or attention to spare for the effectual direction of even a small farm.

Yet if the farm brought scantier profit than it ought to have brought, it was probably no weak solace in the background of a life of harassing interests and perpetual disappointments. Burke was happier at Beaconsfield than anywhere else, and he was happiest there when his house was full of guests. Nothing pleased him better than to drive a visitor over to Windsor, where he would expatiate with enthusiasm "on the proud Keep, rising in the majesty of proportion, and girt with the double belt of its kindred and coeval towers, overseeing and guarding the subjected land." He delighted to point out the house at Uxbridge where Charles I. had carried on the negotiations with the Parliamentary Commissioners; the beautiful grounds of Bulstrode, where Judge Jefferies had once lived; and the church-yard of Beaconsfield, where lay the remains of Edmund Waller, the poet. He was fond of talking of great statesmen—of Walpole, of Pulteney, and of Chatham. Some one had said that Chatham knew nothing whatever except Spenser's *Faery Queen.* "No

matter how that was said," Burke replied to one of his
visitors, "whoever relishes and reads Spenser as he ought
to be read, will have a strong hold of the English language." The delight of the host must have been at least
equalled by the delight of the guest in conversation which
was thus ever taking new turns, branching into topical sur-
prises, and at all turns and on every topic was luminous,
high, edifying, full.

No guest was more welcome than the friend of his boy-
hood; and Richard Shackleton has told how the friendship, cordiality, and openness with which Burke embraced
him was even more than might be expected from long love.
The simple Quaker was confused by the sight of what
seemed to him so sumptuous and worldly a life, and he
went to rest uneasily, doubting whether God's blessing
could go with it. But when he awoke on the morrow of
his first visit, he told his wife, in the language of his sect,
how glad he was " to find no condemnation ; but on the
contrary, ability to put up fervent petitions with much
tenderness on behalf of this great luminary." It is at his
country home that we like best to think of Burke. It is
still a touching picture to the historic imagination to follow him from the heat and violence of the House, where
tipsy squires derided the greatest genius of his time, down
to the calm shades of Beaconsfield, where he would with
his own hands give food to a starving beggar, or medicine
to a peasant sick of the ague ; where he would talk of the
weather, the turnips, and the hay with the team-men and
the farm-bailiff ; and where, in the evening stillness, he
would pace the walk under the trees, and reflect on the
state of Europe and the distractions of his country,

CHAPTER VII.

THE six years which followed the destruction of the Coalition were, in some respects, the most mortifying portion of Burke's troubled career. Pitt was more firmly seated in power than Lord North had ever been, and he used his power to carry out a policy against which it was impossible for the Whigs, on their own principles, to offer an effective resistance. For this is the peculiarity of the King's first victory over the enemies who had done obstinate battle with him for nearly a quarter of a century. He had driven them out of the field, but with the aid of an ally who was as strongly hostile to the royal system as they had ever been. The King had vindicated his right against the Whigs to choose his own ministers; but the new minister was himself a Whig by descent, and a reformer by his education and personal disposition.

Ireland was the subject of the first great battle between the ministry and their opponents. Here, if anywhere, we might have expected from Burke at least his usual wisdom and patience. We saw in a previous chapter (p. 23) what the political condition of Ireland was when Burke went there with Hamilton in 1763. The American war had brought about a great change. The King had shrewdly predicted that if America became free, Ireland would soon

6*

follow the same plan and be a separate state. In fact,
along with the American war we had to encounter an Irish
war also; but the latter was, as an Irish politician called
it at the time, a smothered war. Like the Americans, the
Anglo-Irish entered into non-importation compacts, and
they interdicted commerce. The Irish volunteers, first
forty, then sixty, and at last a hundred thousand strong,
were virtually an army enrolled to overawe the English
ministry and Parliament. Following the spirit, if not the
actual path, of the Americans, they raised a cry for commercial and legislative independence. They were too
strong to be resisted, and in 1782 the Irish Parliament acquired the privilege of initiating and conducting its own
business, without the sanction or control either of the
Privy Council or of the English Parliament. Dazzled by
the chance of acquiring legislative independence, they had
been content with the comparatively small commercial
boons obtained by Lord Nugent and Burke in 1778, and
with the removal of further restrictions by the alarmed
minister in the following year. After the concession of
their independence in 1782, they found that to procure
the abolition of the remaining restrictions on their commerce—the right of trade, for instance, with America and
Africa—the consent of the English legislature was as necessary as it had ever been. Pitt, fresh from the teaching
of Adam Smith and of Shelburne, brought forward in
1785 his famous commercial propositions. The theory of
his scheme was that Irish trade should be free, and that
Ireland should be admitted to a permanent participation
in commercial advantages. In return for this gain, after
her hereditary revenue passed a certain point, she was to
devote the surplus to purposes, such as the maintenance
of the navy, in which the two nations had a common in-

terest. Pitt was to be believed when he declared that, of
all the objects of his political life, this was, in his opinion,
the most important that he had ever engaged in, and he
never expected to meet another that should rouse every
emotion in so strong a degree as this.

A furious battle took place in the Irish Parliament.
There, while nobody could deny that the eleven propositions would benefit the mercantile interests of the country, it was passionately urged that the last of the propositions, that which concerned the apportionment of Irish
revenue to imperial purposes, meant the enslavement of
their unhappy island. Their fetters, they went on, were
clenched, if the English Government was to be allowed
thus to take the initiative in Irish legislation. The factious course pursued by the English Opposition was much
less excusable than the line of the Anglo-Irish leaders.
Fox, who was ostentatiously ignorant of political economy, led the charge. He insisted that Pitt's measures
would annihilate English trade, would destroy the Navi-
gation Laws, and with them would bring our maritime
strength to the ground. Having thus won the favour of
the English manufacturers, he turned round to the Irish
Opposition, and conciliated them by declaring with equal
vehemence that the propositions were an insult to Ireland,
and a nefarious attempt to tamper with her new-born liberties. Burke followed his leader. We may almost say
that for once he allowed his political integrity to be be-
wildered. In 1778 and 1779 he had firmly resisted the
pressure which his mercantile constituents in Bristol had
endeavoured to put upon him ; he had warmly supported
the Irish claims, and had lost his seat in consequence.
The precise ground which he took up in 1785 was this.
He appears to have discerned in Pitt's proposals the germ

of an attempt to extract revenue from Ireland, identical in
purpose, principle, and probable effect with the ever-mem-
orable attempt to extract revenue from the American Colonies.   Whatever stress may be laid upon this, we find it
hard to vindicate Burke from the charge of factiousness.
Nothing can have been more unworthy of him than the
sneer at Pitt in the great speech on the Nabob of Arcot's
debts (1785), for stopping to pick up chaff and straws
from the Irish revenue, instead of checking profligate expenditure in India.

Pitt's alternative was irresistible.   Situated as Ireland
was, she must either be the subservient instrument of
English prosperity, or else she must be allowed to enjoy
the benefits of English trade, taking at the same time
a proportionate share of the common burdens.   Adam
Smith had shown that there was nothing incompatible
with justice in a contribution by Ireland to the public
debt of Great Britain.   That debt, he argued, had been
contracted in support of the government established by
the Revolution ; a government to which the Protestants
of Ireland owed not only the whole authority which they
enjoyed in their own country, but every security which
they possessed for their liberty, property, and religion.
The neighbourhood of Ireland to the shores of the mother
country introduced an element into the problem, which
must have taught every unimpassioned observer that the
American solution would be inadequate for a dependency
that lay at our very door.   Burke could not, in his calmer
moments, have failed to recognize all this.   Yet he lent
himself to the party cry that Pitt was taking his first
measures for the re-enslavement of Ireland.   Had it not
been for what he himself called the delirium of the pre-
ceding session, and which had still not subsided, he would

have seen that Pitt was in truth taking his first measures
for the effective deliverance of Ireland from an unjust
and oppressive subordination. The same delirium committed him to another equally deplorable perversity, when he
opposed, with as many excesses in temper as fallacies in
statesmanship, the wise treaty with France, in which Pitt
partially anticipated the commercial policy of an ampler
treaty three-quarters of a century afterwards.

A great episode in Burke's career now opened. It was
in 1785 that Warren Hastings returned from India, after
a series of exploits as momentous and far-reaching, for
good or evil, as have ever been achieved by any English
ruler. For years Burke had been watching India. With
rising wonder, amazement, and indignation he had steadily
followed that long train of intrigue and crime which had
ended in the consolidation of a new empire. With the
return of Hastings he felt that the time had come for
striking a severe blow and making a signal example. He
gave notice (June, 1785) that he would, at a future day,
make a motion respecting the conduct of a gentleman just
returned from India.

Among minor considerations, we have to remember that
Indian affairs entered materially into the great battle of
parties. It was upon an Indian bill that the late ministry
had made shipwreck. It was notoriously by the aid of po-
tent Indian interests that the new ministry had acquired
a portion of its majority. To expose the misdeeds of
our agents in India was at once to strike the minister
who had dexterously secured their support, and to attack one of the great strongholds of parliamentary corruption. The proceedings against Hastings were, in the
first instance, regarded as a sequel to the struggle over
Fox's East India Bill. That these considerations were

present in Burke's thought there is no doubt, but they
were purely secondary. It was India itself that stood
above all else in his imagination. It had filled his mind
and absorbed his time while Pitt was still an under-gradu-
ate at Cambridge, and Burke was looking forward to match
his plan of economic reform with a greater plan of Indian
reform. In the Ninth Report, the Eleventh Report, and
in his speech on the India Bill of 1783, he had shown both
how thoroughly he had mastered the facts, and how profoundly they had stirred his sense of wrong. The masterpiece known as the Speech on the Nabob of Arcot's debts,
delivered in Parliament on a motion for papers (1785),
handles matters of account, of interest turned into principal, and principal superadded to principal; it deals with
a hundred minute technicalities of teeps and tuncaws, of
gomastahs and soucaring; all with such a suffusion of interest and colour, with such nobility of idea and expression, as could only have come from the addition to genius
of a deep morality of nature and an overwhelming force
of conviction. A space less than one of these pages contains such a picture of the devastation of the Carnatic by
Hyder Ali as may fill the young orator or the young
writer with the same emotions of enthusiasm, emulation,
and despair that torment the artist who first gazes on the
Madonna at Dresden, or the figures of Night and Dawn
and the Penseroso at Florence. The despair is only too
well founded. No conscious study could pierce the secret
of that just and pathetic transition from the havoc of
Hyder Ali to the healing duties of a virtuous government,
to the consolatory celebration of the mysteries of justice
and humanity, to the warning to the unlawful creditors to
silence their inauspicious tongues in presence of the holy
work of restoration, to the generous proclamation against

them that in every country the first creditor is the plough.
The emotions which make the hidden force of such pictures come not by observation. They grow from the sed-
ulous meditation of long years, directed by a powerful intellect and inspired by an interest in human well-being,
which of its own virtue bore the orator into the sustaining
air of the upper gods. Concentrated passion and exhaust-
ive knowledge have never entered into a more formidable
combination. Yet, when Burke made his speech on the
Nabob of Arcot's debts, Pitt and Grenville consulted together whether it was worth answering, and came to the
conclusion that they need not take the trouble.

Neither the scornful neglect of his opponents, nor the
dissuasions of some who sat on his own side, could check
the ardour with which Burke pressed on, as he said, to the
relief of afflicted nations. The fact is, that Burke was not
at all a philanthropist as Clarkson and Wilberforce were
philanthropists. His sympathy was too strongly under
the control of true political reason. In 1780, for instance,
the slave-trade had attracted his attention, and he had even
proceeded to sketch out a code of regulations which provided for its immediate mitigation and ultimate suppression. After mature consideration he abandoned the attempt, from the conviction that the strength of the West
India interest would defeat the utmost efforts of his party.
And he was quite right in refusing to hope from any political action what could only be effected after the moral
preparation of the bulk of the nation. And *direct* moral
or philanthropic apostleship was not his function.

Macaulay, in a famous passage of dazzling lustre and
fine historic colour, describes Burke's holy rage against the
misdeeds of Hastings as due to his sensibility. But sensibility to what? Not merely to those common impressions

of human suffering which kindle the flame of ordinary
philanthropy, always attractive, often so beneficent, but
often so capricious and so laden with secret detriment.
This was no part of Burke's type. Nor is it enough to
say that Burke had what is the distinctive mark of the
true statesman—a passion for good, wise, and orderly government. He had that in the strongest degree. All that
wore the look of confusion he held in abhorrence, and he
detected the seeds of confusion with a penetration that
made other men marvel. He was far too wise a man to
have any sympathy with the energetic exercise of power
for power's sake. He knew well that triumphs of violence
are for the most part little better than temporary make-
shifts, which leave all the work of government to be encountered afterwards by men of essentially greater capacity
than the hero of force without scruple. But he regarded
those whom he called the great bad men of the old stamp,
Cromwell, Richelieu, the Guises, the Condés, with a certain tolerance, because "though the virtues of such men
were not to be taken as a balance to their crimes, yet they
had long views, and sanctified their ambition by aiming at
the orderly rule, and not the destruction of their country."
What he valued was the deep-seated order of systems that
worked by the accepted uses, opinions, beliefs, prejudices
of a community.

This love of right and stable order was not all. That
was itself the growth from a deeper root, partly of conviction and partly of sympathy; the conviction of the rare
and difficult conjunctures of circumstance which are needed for the formation of even the rudest forms of social
union among mankind; and then the sympathy that the
best men must always find it hard to withhold from any
hoary fabric of belief, and any venerated system of gov-

ernment, that has cherished a certain order, and shed even
a ray of the faintest dawn, among the violences and the
darkness of the race.   It was reverence rather than sensibility, a noble and philosophic conservatism rather than
philanthropy, which raised that storm in Burke's breast
against the rapacity of English adventurers in India, and
the imperial crimes of Hastings. Exactly the same tide of
emotion which afterwards filled to the brim the cup of
prophetic anger against the desecrators of the church and
the monarchy of France, now poured itself out against
those who in India had "tossed about, subverted and tore
to pieces, as if it were in the gambols of boyish unlucki-
ness and malice, the most established rights, and the most
ancient and most revered institutions of ages and nations."
From beginning to end of the fourteen years in which
Burke pursued his campaign against Hastings, we see in
every page that the India which ever glowed before his
vision was not the home of picturesque usages and melo-
dramatic costume, but rather, in his own words, the land
of princes once of great dignity, authority, and opulence;
of an ancient and venerable priesthood, the guides of the
people while living, and their consolation in death; of a
nobility of antiquity and renown ; of millions of ingenious
mechanics, and millions of diligent tillers of the earth; and
finally, the land where might be found almost all the re-
ligions professed by men — the Brahminical, the Mussul-
man, the Eastern and the Western Christian.   When he
published his speech on the Nabob of Arcot, Burke pre-
fixed to it an admirable quotation from one of the letters
of the Emperor Julian.   And Julian too, as we all know,
had a strong feeling for the past.   But what in that remarkable figure was only the sentimentalism of reaction,
in Burke was a reasoned and philosophic veneration for all

old and settled order, whether in the free Parliament of
Great Britain, in the ancient absolutism of Versailles, or in
the secular pomp of Oude, and the inviolable sanctity of
Benares, the holy city and the garden of God.

It would be out of place here to attempt to follow the
details of the impeachment. Every reader has heard that
great tale in our history, and everybody knows that it was
Burke's tenacity and power which caused that tale to be
told. The House of Commons would not, it is true, have
directed that Hastings should be impeached, unless Pitt
had given his sanction and approval, and how it was that
Pitt did give his sanction and approval so suddenly and
on grounds ostensibly so slender, remains one of the secrets of history. In no case would the impeachment have
been pressed upon Parliament by the Opposition, and as-
sented to by ministers, if Burke had not been there with
his prodigious industry, his commanding comprehensive
vision, his burning zeal, and his power of kindling in men
so different from him and from one another as Fox, Sheridan, Windham, Grey, a zeal only less intense than his
own.

It was in the spring of 1786 that the articles of charge
of Hastings's high crimes and misdemeanours, as Burke
had drawn them, were presented to the House of Commons.
It was in February, 1788, that Burke opened the vast
cause in the old historic hall at Westminster, in an oration
in which at points he was wound up to such a pitch of
eloquence and passion that every listener, including the
great criminal, held his breath in an agony of horror ; that
women were carried out fainting ; that the speaker himself
became incapable of saying another word, and the specta-
tors of the scene began to wonder whether he would not,
like the mighty Chatham, actually die in the exertion of

his overwhelming powers. Among the illustrious crowd who thronged Westminster Hall in the opening days of the impeachment, was Fanny Burney. She was then in her odious bondage at Court, and was animated by that admiration and pity for Hastings which at Court was the fashion. Windham used to come up from the box of the managers of the impeachment to talk over with her the incidents of the day, and she gave him her impressions of Burke's speech, which were probably those of the majority of his hearers, for the majority were favourable to Hastings. " I told him," says Miss Burney, " that Mr. Burke's opening had struck me with the highest admiration of his powers, from the eloquence, the imagination, the fire, the diversity of expression, and the ready flow of language with which he seemed gifted, in a most superior manner, for any and every purpose to which rhetoric could lead." " And when he came to his two narratives," I continued, " when he related the particulars of those dreadful murders, he interested, he engaged, he at last overpowered me; I felt my cause lost. I could hardly keep on my seat. My eyes dreaded a single glance towards a man so accused as Mr. Hastings; I wanted to sink on the floor, that they might be saved so painful a sight. I had no hope he could clear himself; not another wish in his favour remained. But when from this narration Mr. Burke proceeded to his own comments and declamation—when the charges of rapacity, cruelty, tyranny, were general, and made with all the violence of personal detestation, and continued and aggravated without any further fact or illustration ; then there appeared more of study than of truth, more of invective than of justice; and, in short, so little of proof to so much of passion, that in a very short time I began to lift up my head, my seat was no longer uneasy, my eyes were indifferent which way they looked, or what object caught them, and before I was myself aware of the declension of Mr. Burke's powers over my feelings, I found myself a mere spectator in a public place, and looking all around it, with my opera-glass in my hand !"

In 1795, six years after Burke's opening, the Lords were ready with their verdict/ It had long been anticipated. Hastings was acquitted. This was the close of the fourteen years of labour, from the date of the Select Committee of 1781. "If I were to call for a reward," Burke said, "it would be for the services in which for fourteen years, without intermission, I showed the most industry and had the least success. I mean the affairs of India; they are those on which I value myself the most; most for the importance; most for the labour; most for the judgment; most for constancy and perseverance in the pursuit."

The side that is defeated on a particular issue, is often victorious in the wide and general outcome. Looking back across the ninety years that divide us from that memorable scene in Westminster Hall, we may see that Burke had more success than at first appeared. If he did not convict the man, he overthrew a system, and stamped its principles with lasting censure and shame. Burke had perhaps a silent conviction that it would have been better for us and for India, if Clive had succeeded in his attempt to blow out his own brains in the Madras counting-house, or if the battle of Plassy had been a decisive defeat instead of a decisive victory. "All these circumstances," he once said, in reference to the results of the investigation of the Select Committee, "are not, I confess, very favourable to the idea of our attempting to govern India at all. But there we are: there we are placed by the Sovereign Dis-

poser, and we must do the best we can in our situation.
The situation of man is the preceptor of his duty." If
that situation is better understood now than it was a century ago, and that duty more loftily conceived, the result
is due, so far as such results can ever be due to one man's
action apart from the confluence of the deep impersonal
elements of time, to the seeds of justice and humanity
which were sown by Burke and his associates. Nobody
now believes that Clive was justified in tricking Omichund
by forging another man's name; that Impey was justified
in hanging Nuncomar for committing the very offence for
which Clive was excused or applauded, although forgery
is no grave crime according to Hindoo usage, and it is the
gravest according to English usage; that Hastings did
well in selling English troops to assist in the extermina-
tion of a brave people with whom he was at peace; that
Benfield did well in conniving with an Eastern prince in
a project of extortion against his subjects. The whole
drift of opinion has changed, and it is since the trial of
Hastings that the change has taken place. The question
in Burke's time was whether oppression and corruption
were to continue to be the guiding maxims of English
policy. The personal disinterestedness of the ruler who
had been the chief founder of this policy, and had most
openly set aside all pretence of righteous principle, was
dust in the balance. It was impossible to suppress the
policy without striking a deadly blow at its most eminent
and powerful instrument. That Hastings was acquitted,
was immaterial. The lesson of his impeachment had been
taught with sufficiently impressive force—the great lesson
that Asiatics have rights, and that Europeans have obligations; that a superior race is bound to observe the highest
current morality of the time in all its dealings with the

subject race. Burke is entitled to our lasting reverence as
the first apostle and great upholder of integrity, mercy,
and honour in the relation between his countrymen and
their humble dependents.

He shared the common fate of those who dare to strike
a blow for human justice against the prejudices of national
egotism. But he was no longer able to bear obloquy and
neglect, as he had borne it through the war with the colonies. When he opened the impeachment of Hastings at
Westminster, Burke was very near to his sixtieth year.
Hannah More noted in 1786 that his vivacity had diminished, and that business and politics had impaired his
agreeableness. The simpletons in the House, now that
they had at last found in Pitt a political chief who could
beat the Whig leaders on their own ground of eloquence,
knowledge, and dexterity in debate, took heart as they had
never done under Lord North. They now made deliberate
attempts to silence the veteran by unmannerly and brutal
interruptions, of which a mob of lower class might have
been ashamed. Then suddenly came a moment of such
excitement as has not often been seen in the annals of
party. It became known one day, in the autumn of 1788,
that the King had gone out of his mind.

The news naturally caused the liveliest agitation among
the Whigs. When the severity of the attack forced the
ministry to make preparations for a Regency, the friends
of the Prince of Wales assumed that they would speedily
return to power, and hastened to form their plans accordingly. Fox was travelling in Italy with Mrs. Armitage,
and he had been two months away without hearing a word
from England. The Duke of Portland sent a messenger
in search of him, and after a journey of ten days the messenger found him at Bologna. Fox instantly set off in all

haste for London, which he reached in nine days. The three months that followed were a time of unsurpassed activity and bitterness, and Burke was at least as active and as bitter as the rest of them. He was the writer of the Prince of Wales's letter to Pitt, sometimes set down to Sheridan, and sometimes to Gilbert Elliot. It makes us feel how naturally the style of ideal kingship, its dignity, calm, and high self-consciousness all came to Burke. Although we read of his thus drawing up manifestoes and protests, and deciding minor questions for Fox, which Fox was too irresolute to decide for himself, yet we have it on Burke's own authority that some time elapsed after the return to England before he even saw Fox; that he was not consulted as to the course to be pursued in the grave and difficult questions connected with the Regency; and that he knew as little of the inside of Carlton House, where the Prince of Wales lived, as of Buckingham House, where the King lived. "I mean to continue here," he says to Charles Fox, "until you call upon me; and I find myself perfectly easy, from the implicit confidence that I have in you and the Duke, and the certainty that I am in that you two will do the best for the general advantage of the cause. In that state of mind I feel no desire whatsoever of interfering." Yet the letter itself, and others which follow, testify to the vehemence of Burke's interest in the matter, and to the persistency with which he would have had them follow his judgment, if they would have listened. It is as clear that they did not listen.

Apart from the fierce struggle against Pitt's Regency Bill, Burke's friends were intently occupied with the reconstruction of the Portland cabinet, which the King had so unexpectedly dismissed five years before. This was a sphere in which Burke's gifts were neither required nor

sought. We are rather in distress, Sir Gilbert Elliot
writes, for a proper man for the office of Chancellor of
the Exchequer. "Lord J. Cavendish is very unwilling to
engage again in public affairs. Fox is to be Secretary of
State. Burke, it is thought, would not be approved of,
Sheridan has not the public confidence, and so it comes
down therefore to Grey, Pelham, myself, and perhaps
Windham." Elliot was one of Burke's most faithful and
attached friends, and he was intimately concerned in all
that was going on in the inner circle of the party. It is
worth while, therefore, to reproduce his account, from a
confidential letter to Lady Elliot, of the way in which
Burke's claim to recognition was at this time regarded
and dealt with.

Although I can tell you nothing positive about my own situation,
I was made very happy indeed yesterday by co-operating in the settlement of Burke's, in a manner which gives us great joy as well as
comfort. The Duke of Portland has felt distressed how to arrange
Burke and his family in a manner equal to Burke's merits, and to
the Duke's own wishes, and at the same time so as to be exempt
from the many difficulties which seem to be in the way. He sent
for Pelham and me, as Burke's friends and his own, to advise with
us about it; and we dined yesterday with him and the Duchess, that
we might have time to talk the thing over at leisure and without interruption after dinner. We stayed, accordingly, engaged in that
subject till almost twelve at night, and our conference ended most
happily, and excessively to the satisfaction of us all. The Duke of
Portland has the veneration for Burke that Windham, Pelham, myself, and a few more have, and he thinks it impossible to do too
much for him. He considers the reward to be given to Burke as a
credit and honour to the nation, and he considers the neglect of him
and his embarrassed situation as having been long a reproach to the
country. The unjust prejudice and clamour which has prevailed
against him and his family only determine the Duke the more to do
him justice. The question was how? First, his brother Richard,
who was Secretary to the Treasury before, will have the same office

now, but the Duke intends to give him one of the first offices which
falls vacant, of about 1000*l.* a year for life in the Customs, and he
will then resign the Secretary to the Treasury, which, however, in the
meanwhile is worth 3000*l.* a year. Edmund Burke is to have the
Pay Office, 4000*l.* a year; but as that is precarious and he can leave
no provision for his son, it would, in fact, be doing little or nothing
of any real or substantial value unless some *permanent* provision is
added to it. In this view the Duke is to grant him on the Irish establishment a pension of 2000*l.* a year *clear* for his own life, and the
other half to Mrs. Burke for her life. This will make Burke completely happy, by leaving his wife and son safe from want after his
death, if they should survive him. The Duke's affectionate anxiety
to accomplish this object, and his determination to set all clamour at
defiance on this point of justice, was truly affecting, and increases
my attachment for the Duke. . . . The Duke said the only objection
to this plan was that he thought it was due from this country, and
that he grudged the honour of it to Ireland ; but as nothing in England was ready, this plan was settled. You may think it strange
that to this moment Burke does not know a word of all this, and his
family are indeed, I believe, suffering a little under the apprehension
that he may be neglected in the general scramble. I believe there
never were three cabinet counsellors more in harmony on any subject than we were, nor three people happier in their day's work.[1]

This leaves the apparent puzzle where it was. Why
should Burke not be approved of for Chancellor of the
Exchequer ? What were the many difficulties described as
seeming to be in the way of arranging for Burke, in a
manner equal to Burke's merits and the Duke of Portland's wishes ? His personal relations with the chiefs of
his party were at this time extremely cordial and intimate.
He was constantly a guest at the Duke of Portland's most
private dinner-parties. Fox had gone down to Beaconsfield to recruit himself from the fatigues of his rapid journey from Bologna, and to spend some days in quiet with
Windham and the master of the house. Elliot and Wind-

[1] *Life and Letters of Sir G. Elliot*, i. 261-3.

7

ham, who were talked about for a post for which one of
them says that Burke would not have been approved, vied
with one another in adoring Burke. Finally, Elliot and
the Duke think themselves happy in a day's work which
ended in consigning the man who not only was, but was
admitted to be, the most powerful genius of their party,
to a third-rate post, and that most equivocal distinction, a
pension on the Irish establishment. The common explanation that it illustrates Whig exclusiveness cannot be seriously received as adequate. It is probable, for one thing,
that the feelings of the Prince of Wales had more to do
with it than the feelings of men like the Duke of Portland
or Fox. We can easily imagine how little that most
worthless of human creatures would appreciate the great
qualities of such a man as Burke. The painful fact which
we are unable to conceal from ourselves is, that the common opinion of better men than the Prince of Wales
leaned in the same direction. His violence in the course
of the Regency debates had produced strong disapproval
in the public and downright consternation in his own party. On one occasion he is described by a respectable observer as having " been wilder than ever, and laid himself
and his party more open than ever speaker did. He is
folly personified, but shaking his cap and bells under the
laurel of genius. He finished his wild speech in a manner
next to madness." Moore believes that Burke's indiscre-
tions in these trying and prolonged transactions sowed the
seeds of the alienation between him and Fox two years afterwards. Burke's excited state of mind showed itself in
small things as well as great. Going with Windham to
Carlton House, Burke attacked him in the coach for a difference of opinion about the affairs of a friend, and behaved with such unreasonable passion and such furious

rudeness of manner, that his magnanimous admirer had
some difficulty in obliterating the impression. The public
were less tolerant. Windham has told us that at this time
Burke was a man decried, persecuted, and proscribed, not
being much valued even by his own party, and by half the
nation considered as little better than an ingenious mad-
man.[1] This is evidence beyond impeachment, for Windham loved and honoured Burke with the affection and reverence of a son; and he puts the popular sentiment on
record with grief and amazement. There is other testimony to the same effect. The late Lord Lansdowne, who
must have heard the subject abundantly discussed by those
who were most concerned in it, was once asked by a very
eminent man of our own time why the Whigs kept Burke
out of their cabinets. "Burke!" he cried; "he was so
violent, so overbearing, so arrogant, so intractable, that to
have got on with him in a cabinet would have been utterly
and absolutely impossible."

On the whole, it seems to be tolerably clear that the difficulties in the way of Burke's promotion to high office
were his notoriously straitened circumstances; his ungov-
erned excesses of party zeal and political passion; finally,
what Sir Gilbert Elliot calls the unjust prejudice and clamour against him and his family, and what Burke himself
once called the hunt of obloquy that pursued him all his
life. The first two of these causes can scarcely have op-
erated in the arrangements that were made in the Rockingham and Coalition ministries. But the third, we may
be sure, was incessantly at work. It would have needed
social courage alike in 1782, 1783, and 1788 to give cabinet rank to a man round whose name there floated so
many disparaging associations. Social courage is exactly

[1] Windham's *Diary*, p. 213.

the virtue in which the constructors of a government will always think themselves least able to indulge. Burke, we have to remember, did not stand alone before the world. Elliot describes a dinner-party at Lord Fitzwilliams's, at which four of these half-discredited Irishmen were present. " Burke has now got such a train after him as would sink anybody but himself—his son, who is quite *nauseated* by all mankind; his brother, who is liked better than his son, but is rather offensive with animal spirits and with brogue; and his cousin, Will Burke, who is just returned unexpectedly from India, as much ruined as when he went many years ago, and who is a fresh charge on any prospects of power that Burke may ever have." It was this train, and the ideas of adventurership that clung to them, the inextinguishable stories about papistry and Saint Omer's, the tenacious calumny about the letters of Junius, the notorious circumstances of embarrassment and neediness—it was all these things which combined with Burke's own defects of temper and discretion, to give the Whig grandees as decent a reason as they could have desired for keeping all the great posts of state in their own hands.

It seems difficult to deny that the questions of the Regency had caused the germs of a sort of dissatisfaction and strain in the relations between Fox and Burke. Their feelings to one another have been well compared to the mutual discontent between partners in unsuccessful play, where each suspects that it is the mistakes of the other that lost the game. Whether Burke felt conscious of the failures in discretion and temper, which were the real or pretended excuse for neglect, we cannot tell. There is one passage that reveals a chagrin of this kind. A few days after the meeting between the Duke of Portland and Elliot, for the purpose of settling his place in the new ministry, Burke went down to Beaconsfield. In writing (January 24th, 1789) to invite Windham and Pelham to come to stay a night, with promise of a leg of mutton cooked by a dairy-maid who was not a bad hand at a pinch, he goes on to say that his health has received some small benefit from his journey to the country. "But this view to health, though far from unnecessary to me, was not the chief cause of my present retreat. I began to find that I was grown rather too anxious; and had begun to discover to myself and to others a solicitude relative to the present state of affairs, which, though their strange condition might well warrant it in others, is certainly less suitable to my time of life, in which all emotions are less allowed; and to which, most certainly, all human concerns ought in reason to become more indifferent, than to those who have work to do, and a good deal of day, and of inexhausted strength, to do it in."[1]

The King's unexpected restoration to health two or three weeks later, brought to nought all the hope and ambition of the Whigs, and confirmed Pitt in power for the rest of Burke's lifetime. But an event now came to pass in the world's history which transformed Burke in an instant from a man decried, persecuted, proscribed, into an object of exultant adoration all over Europe.

[1] *Correspondence*, iii. 89.

CHAPTER VIII.

THE FRENCH REVOLUTION.

WE have now come to the second of the two momentous changes in the world's affairs, in which Burke played an imposing and historic part. His attitude in the first of them, the struggle for American independence, commands almost without alloy the admiration and reverence of posterity. His attitude in the second of them, the great revolution in France, has raised controversies which can only be compared in heat and duration to the master controversies of theology. If the history of society were written as learned men write the history of the Christian faith and its churches, Burke would figure in the same strong prominence, whether deplorable or glorious, as Arius and Athanasius, Augustine and Sabellius, Luther and Ignatius. If we ask how it is that now, nearly a century after the event, men are still discussing Burke's pamphlet on the Revolution as they are still discussing Bishop Butler's *Analogy*, the answer is that in one case as in the other the questions at issue are still unsettled, and that Burke offers in their highest and most comprehensive form all the considerations that belong to one side of the dispute. He was not of those of whom Coleridge said that they proceeded with much solemnity to solve the riddle of the French Revolution by anecdotes. He suspended it in the same light of great social ideas and wide principles, in which its authors and champions professed to represent it. Unhappily he advanced from criticism to practical exhortation, in our opinion the most mischievous and indefensible that has ever been pressed by any statesman on any nation. But the force of the criticism remains, its foresight remains, its commemoration of valuable elements of life which men were forgetting, its discernment of the limitations of things, its sense of the awful emergencies of the problem. When our grandchildren have made up their minds, once for all, as to the merits of the social transformation which dawned on Europe in 1789, then Burke's *Reflections* will become a mere literary antiquity, and not before.

From the very beginning Burke looked upon the proceedings in France with distrust. He had not a moment of enthusiasm or sympathy of which to repent. When the news reached England that the insurgents of Paris had stormed the Bastille, Fox exclaimed with exultation, how much it was the greatest event that had ever happened in the world, how much the best. Is it an infirmity to wish, for an instant, that some such phrase of generous hope had escaped from Burke; that he had for a day or an hour undergone that fine illusion which was lighted up in the spirits of men like Wordsworth and Coleridge? Those great poets, who were destined one day to preach even a wiser and a loftier conservatism than his own, have told us what they felt—

> When France in wrath her giant limbs upreared,
> And with that oath, which smote air, earth, and sea,
> Stamped her strong foot, and said she would be free.

Burke from the first espied the looming shadow of a catastrophe. In August he wrote to Lord Charlemont

that the events in France had something paradoxical and
mysterious about them; that the outbreak of the old Parisian ferocity might be no more than a sudden explosion,
but if it should happen to be *character* rather than accident, then the people would need a strong hand like that
of their former masters to coerce them; that all depended
upon the French having wise heads among them, and upon
these wise heads, if such there were, acquiring an authority
to match their wisdom. There is nothing here but a calm
and sagacious suspense of judgment. It soon appeared
that the old Parisian ferocity was still alive. In the events
of October, 1789, when the mob of Paris marched out
to Versailles and marched back again with the King and
Queen in triumphal procession, Burke felt in his heart that
the beginning of the end had come, and that the catastrophe was already at hand. In October he wrote a long letter to the French gentleman to whom he afterwards addressed the *Reflections*. " You hope, sir," he said, " that I
think the French deserving of liberty. I certainly do. I
certainly think that all men who desire it deserve it. We
cannot forfeit our right to it, but by what forfeits our title
to the privileges of our kind. The liberty I mean is *social*
freedom. It is that state of things in which liberty is secured by equality of restraint. This kind of liberty is, indeed, but another name for justice. *Whenever a separation
is made between liberty and justice, neither is in my opinion
safe.*" The weightiest and most important of all political
truths, and worth half the fine things that poets have sung
about freedom—if it could only have been respected, how
different the course of the Revolution! But the engineer
who attempts to deal with the abysmal rush of the falls
of Niagara must put aside the tools that constructed the
Bridgewater Canal and the Chelsea Waterworks. Nobody

recognised so early as Burke that France had really embarked among cataracts and boiling gulfs, and the pith
of all his first criticisms, including the *Reflections,* was
the proposition that to separate freedom from justice was
nothing else than to steer the ship of state direct into the
Maelstrom.   It is impossible to deny that this was true.
Unfortunately it was a truth which the wild spirits that
were then abroad in the storm made of no avail.

Destiny aimed an evil stroke when Burke, whose whole
soul was bound up in order, peace, and gently enlarged
precedent, found himself face to face with the portentous
man-devouring Sphinx. He, who could not endure that a
few clergymen should be allowed to subscribe to the Bible
instead of to the Articles, saw the ancient Church of Chris-
tendom prostrated, its possessions confiscated, its priests
proscribed, and Christianity itself officially superseded.
The economical reformer, who when his zeal was hottest
declined to discharge a tide-waiter or a scullion in the
royal kitchen, who should have acquired the shadow of a
vested interest in his post, beheld two great orders stripped
of their privileges and deprived of much of their lands,
though their possession had been sanctified by the express
voice of the laws and the prescription of many centuries.
He, who was full of apprehension and anger at the proposal to take away a member of Parliament from St. Mi-
chael's or Old Sarum, had to look on while the most august monarchy in Europe was overturned.   The man who
dreaded fanatics, hated atheists, despised political theorisers, and was driven wild at the notion of applying metaphysical rights and abstract doctrines to public affairs, suddenly beheld a whole kingdom given finally up to fanatics, atheists, and theorisers, who talked of nothing but the
rights of man, and deliberately set as wide a gulf as ruin

7*

and bloodshed could make between themselves and every
incident or institution in the history of their land. The
statesman who had once declared, and habitually proved,
his preference for peace over even truth, who had all his
life surrounded himself with a mental paradise of order
and equilibrium, in a moment found himself confronted by
the stupendous and awful spectre which a century of disorder had raised in its supreme hour. It could not have
been difficult for any one who had studied Burke's character and career, to foretell all that now came to pass with
him.

It was from an English, and not from a French point
of view, that Burke was first drawn to write upon the
Revolution. The 4th of November was the anniversary
of the landing of the Prince of Orange, and the first act
in the Revolution of 1688. The members of an association which called itself the Revolution Society, chiefly
composed of Dissenters, but not without a mixture of
Churchmen, including a few peers and a good many members of the House of Commons, met as usual to hear a
sermon in commemoration of the glorious day. Dr.
Price was the preacher, and both in the morning sermon
and in the speeches which followed in the festivities of
the afternoon the French were held up to the loudest admiration, as having carried the principles of our own
Revolution to a loftier height, and having opened bound-
less hopes to mankind. By these harmless proceedings
Burke's anger and scorn were aroused to a pitch which
must seem to us, as it seemed to not a few of his contemporaries, singularly out of all proportion to its cause.
Deeper things were doubtless in silent motion within him.
He set to work upon a denunciation of Price's doctrines,
with a velocity that reminds us of Aristotle's comparison

of anger to the over-hasty servant, who runs off with all speed before he has listened to half the message. This was the origin of the *Reflections*. The design grew as the writer went on. His imagination took fire ; his memory quickened a throng of impressive associations ; his excited vision revealed to him a band of vain, petulant upstarts persecuting the ministers of a sacred religion, insulting a virtuous and innocent sovereign, and covering with humiliation the august daughter of the Cæsars ; his mind teemed with the sage maxims of the philosophy of things established, and the precepts of the gospel of order. Every courier that crossed the Channel supplied new material to his contempt and his alarm. He condemned the whole method and course of the French reforms. His judgment was in suspense no more. He no longer distrusted ; he hated, despised, and began to dread.

Men soon began to whisper abroad that Burke thought ill of what was going on over the water. When it transpired that he was writing a pamphlet, the world of letters was stirred with the liveliest expectation. The name of the author, the importance of the subject, and the singularity of his opinions, so Mackintosh informs us, all inflamed the public curiosity. Soon after Parliament met for the session (1790), the army estimates were brought up. Fox criticised the increase of our forces, and incidentally hinted something in praise of the French army, which had shown that a man could be a soldier without ceasing to be a citizen. Some days afterwards the subject was revived, and Pitt, as well as Fox, avowed himself hopeful of the good effect of the Revolution upon the order and government of France. Burke followed in a very different vein, openly proclaiming that dislike and fear of the Revolution which was to be the one ceaseless refrain of all that he spoke or wrote for the rest of his life. He deplored Fox's praise of the army for breaking their lawful allegiance, and then he proceeded with ominous words to the effect that, if any friend of his should concur in any measures which should tend to introduce such a democracy as that of France, he would abandon his best friends and join with his worst enemies to oppose either the means or the end. This has unanimously been pronounced one of the most brilliant and effective speeches that Burke ever made. Fox rose with distress on every feature, and made the often-quoted declaration of his debt to Burke: "If all the political information I have learned from books, all which I have gained from science, and all which my knowledge of the world and its affairs has taught me, were put into one scale, and the improvement which I have derived from my right honourable friend's instruction and conversation were placed in the other, I should be at a loss to decide to which to give the preference. I have learnt more from my right honourable friend than from all the men with whom I ever conversed." All seemed likely to end in a spirit of conciliation, until Sheridan rose, and in the plainest terms that he could find expressed his dissent from everything that Burke had said. Burke immediately renounced his friendship. For the first time in his life he found the sympathy of the House vehemently on his side.

In the following month (March, 1790) this unpromising incident was succeeded by an aberration which no rational man will now undertake to defend. Fox brought forward a motion for the repeal of the Test and Corporation Acts. He did this in accordance with a recent suggestion of Burke's own, that he should strengthen his political position by winning the support of the Dissenters.

Burke himself had always denounced the Test Act as bad, and as an abuse of sacred things. To the amazement of everybody, and to the infinite scandal of his party, he now pronounced the Dissenters to be disaffected citizens, and refused to relieve them. Well might Fox say that Burke's words had filled him with grief and shame.

Meanwhile the great rhetorical fabric gradually arose. Burke revised, erased, moderated, strengthened, emphasized, wrote and re-wrote with indefatigable industry. With the manuscript constantly under his eyes, he lingered busily, pen in hand, over paragraphs and phrases, antitheses and apophthegms. The *Reflections* was no superb improvisation. Its composition recalls Palma Giovine's account of the mighty Titian's way of working; how the master made his preparations with resolute strokes of a heavily-laden brush, and then turned his picture to the wall, and by-and-by resumed again, and then again and again, re-dressing, adjusting, modelling the light with a rub of his finger, or dabbing a spot of dark colour into some corner with a touch of his thumb, and finally working all his smirches, contrasts, abruptnesses, into the glorious harmony that we know. Burke was so unwearied in this insatiable correction and alteration, that the printer found it necessary, instead of making the changes marked upon the proof-sheets, to set up the whole in type afresh. The work was upon the easel for exactly a year. It was November (1790) before the result came into the hands of the public. It was a small octavo of three hundred and fifty-six pages, in contents rather less than twice the present volume, bound in an unlettered wrapper of grey paper, and sold for five shillings. In less than twelve months it reached its eleventh edition, and it has been computed that not many short of thirty thousand copies were sold within the next six years.

The first curiosity had languished in the course of the long delay, but it was revived in its strongest force when the book itself appeared. A remarkable effect instantly followed. Before the *Reflections* was published, the predominant sentiment in England had been one of mixed astonishment and sympathy. Pitt had expressed this common mood both in the House of Commons and in private. It was impossible for England not to be amazed at the uprising of a nation whom they had been accustomed to think of as willing slaves, and it was impossible for her, when the scene did not happen to be the American colonies or Ireland, not to profess good wishes for the cause of emancipation all over the world. Apart from the natural admiration of a free people for a neighbour struggling to be free, England saw no reason to lament a blow to a sovereign and a government who had interfered on the side of her insurgent colonies. To this easy state of mind Burke's book put an immediate end. At once, as contemporaries assure us, it divided the nation into two parties. On both sides it precipitated opinion. With a long-resounding blast on his golden trumpet Burke had unfurled a new flag, and half the nation hurried to rally to it—that half which had scouted his views on America, which had bitterly disliked his plan of Economic Reform, which had mocked his ideas on religious toleration, and which a moment before had hated and reviled him beyond all men living, for his fierce tenacity in the impeachment of Warren Hastings. The King said to everybody who came near him that the book was a good book, a very good book, and every gentleman ought to read it. The universities began to think of offering the scarlet gown of their most honourable degree to the assailant of Price and the Dissenters. The great army of the indolent good, the people who lead excellent lives and never use their reason, took violent alarm. The timorous, the weak-minded, the bigoted, were suddenly awakened to a sense of what they owed to themselves. Burke gave them the key which enabled them to interpret the Revolution in harmony with their usual ideas and their temperament.

Reaction quickly rose to a high pitch. One preacher in a parish church in the neighbourhood of London celebrated the anniversary of the Restoration of King Charles II. by a sermon, in which the pains of eternal damnation were confidently promised to political disaffection. Romilly, mentioning to a friend that the *Reflections* had got into a fourteenth edition, wondered whether Burke was not rather ashamed of his success. It is when we come to the rank and file of reaction that we find it hard to forgive the man of genius who made himself the organ of their selfishness, their timidity, and their blindness. We know, alas! that the parts of his writings on French affairs to which they would fly were not likely to be the parts which calm men now read with sympathy, but the scoldings, the screamings, the unworthy vituperation with which, especially in the latest of them, he attacked everybody who took part in the Revolution, from Condorcet and Lafayette down to Marat and Couthon. It was the feet of clay that they adored in their image, and not the head of fine gold and the breasts and the arms of silver.

On the continent of Europe the excitement was as great among the ruling classes as it was at home. Mirabeau, who had made Burke's acquaintance some years before in England, and even been his guest at Beaconsfield, now made the *Reflections* the text of more than one tremen-

dous philippic. Louis XVI. is said to have translated the
book into French with his own hand. Catherine of
Russia, Voltaire's adored Semiramis of the North, the
benefactress of Diderot, the ready helper of the philosophic party, pressed her congratulations on the great
pontiff of the old order, who now thundered anathema
against the philosophers and all their works.

It is important to remember the stage which the Revolution had reached when Burke was composing his attack
upon it. The year 1790 was precisely the time when the
hopes of the best men in France shone most brightly, and
seemed most reasonable. There had been disorders, and
Paris still had ferocity in her mien. But Robespierre was
an obscure figure on the back benches of the Assembly.
Nobody had ever heard of Danton. The name of Republic had never been so much as whispered. The King still
believed that constitutional monarchy would leave him as
much power as he desired. He had voluntarily gone to
the National Assembly, and in simple language had ex-
horted them all to imitate his example by professing the
single opinion, the single interest, the single wish—attachment to the new constitution, and ardent desire for the
peace and happiness of France. The clergy, it is true,
were violently irritated by the spoliation of their goods,
and the nobles had crossed the Rhine, to brood impotent-
ly in the safety of Coblenz over projects of a bloody re-
venge upon their country. But France, meanwhile, paid
little heed either to the anger of the clergy or the menaces
of the emigrant nobles, and at the very moment when
Burke was writing his most sombre pages, Paris and the
provinces were celebrating with transports of joy and enthusiasm the civic oath, the federation, the restoration of
concord to the land, the final establishment of freedom

and justice in a regenerated France. This was the happy
scene over which Burke suddenly stretched out the right
arm of an inspired prophet, pointing to the cloud of thunder and darkness that was gathering on the hills, and proclaiming to them the doom that had been written upon
the wall by the fingers of an inexorable hand. It is no
wonder that when the cloud burst and the doom was fulfilled, men turned to Burke, as they went of old to Ahith-
ophel, whose counsel was as if a man had inquired of the
oracle of God.

It is not to our purpose to discuss all the propositions
advanced in the *Reflections*, much less to reply to them.
The book is like some temple, by whose structure and design we allow ourselves to be impressed, without being
careful to measure the precise truth or fitness of the worship to which it was consecrated by its first founders.
Just as the student of the *Politics* of Aristotle may well
accept all the wisdom of it, without caring to protest at
every turn against slavery as the basis of a society, so we
may well cherish all the wisdom of the *Reflections*, at this
distance of time, without marking as a rubric on every
page that half of these impressive formulæ and inspiring
declamations were irrelevant to the occasion which called
them forth, and exercised for the hour an influence that
was purely mischievous. Time permits to us this profita-
ble lenity. In reading this, the first of his invectives, it
is important for the sake of clearness of judgment to put
from our minds the practical policy which Burke afterwards so untiringly urged upon his countrymen. As yet
there is no exhortation to England to interfere, and we
still listen to the voice of the statesman, and are not deaf-
ened by the passionate cries of the preacher of a crusade.
When Burke wrote the *Reflections*, he was justified in crit-

icising the Revolution as an extraordinary movement, but
still a movement professing to be conducted on the principles of rational and practicable politics. They were the
principles to which competent onlookers like Jefferson
and Morris had expected the Assembly to conform, but to
which the Assembly never conformed for an instant. It
was on the principles of rational politics that Fox and
Sheridan admired it. On these principles Burke condemned it. He declared that the methods of the Constituent Assembly, up to the summer of 1790, were unjust,
precipitate, destructive, and without stability. Men had
chosen to build their house on the sands, and the winds
and the seas would speedily beat against it and overthrow it.

His prophecy was fulfilled to the letter. What is still
more important for the credit of his foresight is, that not
only did his prophecy come true, but it came true for the
reasons that he had fixed upon. It was, for instance, the
constitution of the Church, in which Burke saw the worst
of the many bad mistakes of the Assembly. History, now
slowly shaking herself free from the passions of a century, agrees that the civil constitution of the clergy was the
measure which, more than any other, decisively put an end
to whatever hopes there might have been of a peaceful
transition from the old order to the new. A still more
striking piece of foresight is the prediction of the despotism of the Napoleonic Empire. Burke had compared the
levelling policy of the Assembly in their geometrical division of the departments, and their isolation from one another of the bodies of the state, to the treatment which a
conquered country receives at the hands of its conquerors.
Like Romans in Greece or Macedon, the French innovators
had destroyed the bonds of union, under color of provid-

ing for the independence of each of their cities. "If the
present project of a Republic should fail," Burke said, with
a prescience really profound, "all securities to a moderate freedom fail with it. All the indirect restraints which
mitigate despotism are removed; insomuch that, if monarchy should ever again obtain an entire ascendancy in
France under this or any other dynasty, it will probably
be, if not voluntarily tempered at setting out by the wise
and virtuous counsels of the prince, the most completely
arbitrary power that ever appeared on earth." Almost at
the same moment Mirabeau was secretly writing to the
King, that their plan of reducing all citizens to a single
class would have delighted Richelieu. This equal surface,
he said, facilitates the exercise of power, and many reigns
in an absolute government would not have done as much
as this single year of revolution for the royal authority.
Time showed that Burke and Mirabeau were right.

History ratifies nearly all Burke's strictures on the levity and precipitancy of the first set of actors in the revolutionary drama. No part of the *Reflections* is more energetic than the denunciation of geometric and literary
methods; and these are just what the modern explorer
hits upon, as one of the fatal secrets of the catastrophe.
De Tocqueville's chapter on the causes which made literary
men the principal persons in France, and the effect which
this had upon the Revolution (Bk. III. ch. i.), is only a little too cold to be able to pass for Burke's own. Quinet's
work on the Revolution is one long sermon, full of eloquence and cogency, upon the incapacity and blindness of
the men who undertook the conduct of a tremendous crisis upon mere literary methods, without the moral courage to obey the logic of their beliefs, with the student's
ignorance of the eager passion and rapid imagination of

multitudes of men, with the pedant's misappreciation of a
people, of whom it has been said by one of themselves
that there never was a nation more led by its sensations,
and less by its principles. Comte, again, points impressively to the Revolution as the period which illustrates
more decisively than another the peril of confounding the
two great functions of speculation and political action;
and he speaks with just reprobation of the preposterous
idea in the philosophic politicians of the epoch, that society was at their disposal, independent of its past develop-
ment, devoid of inherent impulses, and easily capable of
being morally regenerated by the mere modification of legislative rules.

What then was it that, in the midst of so much per-
spicacity as to detail, blinded Burke, at the time when he
wrote the *Reflections*, to the true nature of the movement?
Is it not this, that he judges the Revolution as the solution of a merely political question? If the Revolution
had been merely political, his judgment would have been
adequate. The question was much deeper. It was a social question that burned under the surface of what seemed no more than a modification of external arrangements.
That Burke was alive to the existence of social problems,
and that he was even tormented by them, we know from
an incidental passage in the *Reflections*. There he tells
us how often he had reflected, and never reflected without
feeling, upon the innumerable servile and degrading occu-
pations to which, by the social economy, so many wretches
are inevitably doomed. He had pondered whether there
could be any means of rescuing these unhappy people
from their miserable industry, without disturbing the natural course of things, and impeding the great wheel of circulation which is turned by their labour. This is the vein

of that striking passage in his first composition, which I have already quoted (p. 16). Burke did not yet see, and probably never saw, that one key to the events which astonished and exasperated him, was simply that the persons most urgently concerned had taken the riddle which perplexed him into their own hands, and had in fiery earnest set about their own deliverance. The pith of the Revolution, up to 1790, was less the political constitution, of which Burke says so much, and so much that is true, but the social and economic transformation, of which he says so little. It was not a question of the power of the King, or the measure of an electoral circumscription, that made the Revolution; it was the iniquitous distribution of the taxes, the scourge of the militia service, the scourge of the road service, the destructive tyranny exercised in the vast preserves of wild game, the vexatious rights and imposts of the lords of manors, and all the other odious burdens and heavy impediments on the prosperity of the thrifty and industrious part of the nation. If he had seen ever so clearly that one of the most important sides of the Revolution in progress was the rescue of the tiller of the soil, Burke would still doubtless have viewed events with bitter suspicion. For the process could not be executed without disturbing the natural course of things, and without violating his principle that all changes should find us with our minds tenacious of justice and tender of property. A closer examination than he chose to give, of the current administration alike of justice and of property under the old system, would have explained to him that an hour had come in which the spirit of property and of justice compelled a supersession of the letter.

If Burke had insisted on rigidly keeping sensibility to the wrongs of the French people out of the discussion, on

the ground that the whole subject was one for positive
knowledge and logical inference, his position would have
been intelligible and defensible.   He followed no such
course.   His pleading turns constantly to arguments from
feeling; but it is always to feeling on one side, and to a
sensibility that is only alive to the concentrated force of
historic associations.   How much pure and uncontrolled
emotion had to do with what ought to have been the reasoned judgments of his understanding, we know on his
ówn evidence.   He had sent the proof-sheets of a part of
his book to Sir Philip Francis.   They contained the famous passage describing the French Queen as he had seen
her seventeen years before at Versailles.   Francis bluntly
wrote to him that, in his opinion, all Burke's eloquence
about Marie Antoinette was no better than pure foppery,
and he referred to the Queen herself as no better than
Messalina.   Burke was so excited by this that his son, in a
rather officious letter, begged Francis not to repeat such
stimulating remonstrance.   What is interesting in the incident is Burke's own reply.   He knew nothing, he said,
of the story of Messalina, and declined the obligation of
proving judicially the virtues of all those whom he saw
suffering wrong and contumely, before he endeavoured to
interest others in their sufferings, and before endeavouring
to kindle horror against midnight assassins at backstairs
and their more wicked abettors in pulpits.   And then he
went on, " I tell you again that the recollection of the
manner in which I saw the Queen of France in the year
1774 [1773], and the contrast between that brilliancy,
splendour, and beauty, with the prostrate homage of a
nation to her, and the abominable scene of 1789 which
I was describing, *did* draw tears from me and wetted
my paper.   These tears came again into my eyes al-

most as often as I looked at the description—they may again."

The answer was obvious. It was well to pity the un-merited agonies of Marie Antoinette, though as yet, we must remember, she had suffered nothing beyond the in-dignities of the days of October at Versailles. But did not the protracted agonies of a nation deserve the tribute of a tear? As Paine asked, were men to weep over the plumage, and forget the dying bird? The bulk of the people must labour, Burke told them, "to obtain what by labour can be obtained; and when they find, as they com-monly do, the success disproportioned to the endeavour, they must be taught their consolation in the final propor-tions of eternal justice." When we know that a Lyons silk-weaver, working as hard as he could for over seventeen hours a day, could not earn money enough to procure the most bare and urgent necessaries of subsistence, we may know with what benignity of brow eternal justice must have presented herself in the garret of that hapless wretch. It was no idle abstraction, no metaphysical right of man, for which the French cried, but only the practical right of being permitted, by their own toil, to save themselves and the little ones about their knees from hunger and cruel death. The *mainmortable* serfs of ecclesiastics are vari-ously said to have been a million and a million and a half at the time of the Revolution. Burke's horror, as he thought of the priests and prelates who left palaces and dignities to earn a scanty living by the drudgery of teach-ing their language in strange lands, should have been alle-viated by the thought that a million or more of men were rescued from ghastly material misery. Are we to be so overwhelmed with sorrow over the pitiful destiny of the men of exalted rank and sacred function, as to have no

tears for the forty thousand serfs in the gorges of the
Jura, who were held in dead-hand by the Bishop of Saint-
Claude?

The simple truth is that Burke did not know enough of
the subject about which he was writing. When he said,
for instance, that the French before 1789 possessed all the
elements of a constitution that might be made nearly as
good as could be wished, he said what many of his contemporaries knew, and what all subsequent investigation
and meditation have proved, to be recklessly ill-considered
and untrue. As to the social state of France, his information was still worse. He saw the dangers and disorders
of the new system, but he saw a very little way indeed
into the more cruel dangers and disorders of the old.
Mackintosh replied to the *Reflections* with manliness and
temperance in the *Vindiciæ Gallicæ*. Thomas Paine replied to them with an energy, courage, and eloquence worthy of his cause, in the *Rights of Man*. But the substantial and decisive reply to Burke came from his former
correspondent, the farmer at Bradfield, in Suffolk. Arthur
Young published his *Travels in France* some eighteen
months after the *Reflections* (1792), and the pages of the
twenty-first chapter, in which he closes his performance,
as a luminous criticism of the most important side of the
Revolution, are worth a hundred times more than Burke,
Mackintosh, and Paine all put together. Young afterwards became panic-stricken, but his book remained. There
the writer plainly enumerates without trope or invective
the intolerable burdens under which the great mass of the
French people had for long years been groaning. It was
the removal of these burdens that made the very heart's
core of the Revolution, and gave to France that new life
which so soon astonished and terrified Europe. Yet

Burke seems profoundly unconscious of the whole of them. He even boldly asserts that, when the several orders met in their bailliages in 1789, to choose their representatives and draw up their grievances and instructions, in no one of these instructions did they charge, or even hint at, any of those things which had drawn upon the usurping Assembly the detestation of the rational part of mankind. He could not have made a more enormous blunder. There was not a single great change made by the Assembly which had not been demanded in the lists of grievances that had been sent up by the nation to Versailles. The division of the kingdom into districts, and the proportioning of the representation to taxes and population; the suppression of the intendants; the suppression of all monks, and the sale of their goods and estates; the abolition of feudal rights, duties, and services; the alienation of the King's domains; the demolition of the Bastille; these and all else were in the prayers of half the petitions that the country had laid at the feet of the King.

If this were merely an incidental blunder in a fact, it might be of no importance. But it was a blunder which went to the very root of the discussion. The fact that France was now at the back of the Assembly, inspiring its counsels and ratifying its decrees, was the cardinal element, and that is the fact which at this stage Burke systematically ignored. That he should have so ignored it, left him in a curious position, for it left him without any rational explanation of the sources of the policy which kindled his indignation and contempt. A publicist can never be sure of his position, until he can explain to himself even what he does not wish to justify to others. Burke thought it enough to dwell upon the immense number of lawyers in the Assembly, and to show that

8

lawyers are naturally bad statesmen. He did not look
the state of things steadily in the face. It was no easy
thing to do. But Burke was a man who ought to have
done it. He set all down to the ignorance, folly, and
wickedness of the French leaders. This was as shallow
as the way in which his enemies, the philosophers, used
to set down the superstition of eighteen centuries to the
craft of priests, and all defects in the government of Europe to the cruelty of tyrants. How it came about that
priests and tyrants acquired their irresistible power over
men's minds, they never inquired. And Burke never inquired into the enthusiastic acquiescence of the nation,
and, what was most remarkable of all, the acquiescence of
the army, in the strong measures of the Assembly. Burke
was, in truth, so appalled by the magnitude of the enter-
prise on which France had embarked, that he utterly forgot for once the necessity in political affairs, of seriously
understanding the originating conditions of things. He
was strangely content with the explanations that came
from the malignants at Coblenz, and he actually told
Francis that he charged the disorders not on the mob,
but on the Duke of Orleans and Mirabeau, on Barnave
and Bailly, on Lameth and Lafayette, who had spent immense sums of money, and used innumerable arts, to stir
up the populace throughout France to the commission of
the enormities that were shocking the conscience of Europe. His imagination broke loose. His practical reason
was mastered by something that was deeper in him than
reason.

This brings me to remark a really singular trait. In
spite of the predominance of practical sagacity, of the
habits and spirit of public business, of vigorous actuality
in Burke's character, yet at the bottom of all his thoughts

about communities and governments there lay a certain mysticism. It was no irony, no literary trope, when he talked of our having taught the American husbandman "piously to believe in the mysterious virtue of wax and parchment." He was using no otiose epithet, when he described the disposition of a stupendous wisdom, "moulding together the great mysterious incorporation of the human race." To him there actually was an element of mystery in the cohesion of men in societies, in political obedience, in the sanctity of contract; in all that fabric of law and charter and obligation, whether written or unwritten, which is the sheltering bulwark between civilization and barbarism. When reason and history had contributed all that they could to the explanation, it seemed to him as if the vital force, the secret of organization, the binding framework, must still come from the impenetrable regions beyond reasoning and beyond history. There was another great conservative writer of that age, whose genius was aroused into a protest against the revolutionary spirit, as vehement as Burke's. This was Joseph de Maistre, one of the most learned, witty, and acute of all reactionary philosophers. De Maistre wrote a book on the Generative Principle of Political Constitutions. He could only find this principle in the operation of occult and supernatural forces, producing the half-divine legislators who figure mysteriously in the early history of nations. Hence he held, and with astonishing ingenuity enforced, the doctrine that nothing else could deliver Europe from the Satanic forces of revolution—he used the word Satanic in all literal seriousness—save the divinely inspired supremacy of the Pope. No natural operations seemed at all adequate either to produce or to maintain the marvel of a coherent society. We are reminded of a professor who, in the fantastic days of geol-

ogy, explained the Pyramids of Egypt to be the remains
of a volcanic eruption, which had forced its way upwards
by a slow and stately motion; the hieroglyphs were crys-
talline formations; and the shaft of the great Pyramid
was the air-hole of a volcano. De Maistre preferred a similar explanation of the monstrous structures of modern
society. The hand of man could never have reared, and
could never uphold them. If we cannot say that Burke
laboured in constant travail with the same perplexity, it is
at least true that he was keenly alive to it, and that one of
the reasons why he dreaded to see a finger laid upon a
single stone of a single political edifice, was his conscious-
ness that he saw no answer to the perpetual enigma how
any of these edifices had ever been built, and how the passion, violence, and waywardness of the natural man had
ever been persuaded to bow their necks to the strong yoke
of a common social discipline. Never was mysticism more
unseasonable; never was an hour when men needed more
carefully to remember Burke's own wise practical precept,
when he was talking about the British rule in India, that
we must throw a sacred veil over the beginnings of government. Many woes might perhaps have been saved to
Europe, if Burke had applied this maxim to the government of the new France.

Much has always been said about the inconsistency between Burke's enmity to the Revolution, and his enmity
to Lord North in one set of circumstances, and to Warren
Hastings in another. The pamphleteers of the day made
selections from the speeches and tracts of his happier time,
and the seeming contrast had its effect. More candid opponents admitted then, as all competent persons admit
now, that the inconsistency was merely verbal and superficial. Watson, the Bishop of Llandaff, was only one of

many who observed very early that this was the unmistakable temper of Burke's mind. " I admired, as everybody did," he said, " the talents, but not the principles of Mr. Burke ; his opposition to the Clerical Petition [for relaxation of subscription, 1772], first excited my suspicion of his being a High-Churchman in religion, and a Tory, perhaps an aristocratic Tory, in the state." Burke had, indeed, never been anything else than a conservative. He was like Falkland, who had bitterly assailed Strafford and Finch on the same principles on which, after the outbreak of the civil war, he consented to be secretary of state to King Charles. Coleridge is borne out by a hundred passages, when he says that in Burke's writings at the beginning of the American Revolution and in those at the beginning of the French Revolution, the principles are the same and the deductions are the same ; the practical inferences are almost opposite in the one case from those drawn in the other, yet in both equally legitimate. It would be better to say that they would have been equally legitimate, if  Burke had been as right in his facts, and as ample in his knowledge in the case of France, as he was in the case of America. We feel, indeed, that, partly from want of this knowledge, he has gone too far from some of the wise maxims of an earlier time. What has become of the doctrine that all great public collections of men—he was then speaking of the House of Commons—" possess a marked love of virtue and an abhorrence of vice."[1] Why was the French Assembly not to have the benefit of this admirable generalisation ? What has become of all those sayings about the presumption, in all disputes between nations and rulers, " being at least upon a par in favour of the people ;" and a populace never rebelling from passion for attack, but

[1] *American Taxation.*

from impatience of suffering? And where is now that
strong dictum, in the letter to the Sheriffs of Bristol, that
"general rebellions and revolts of a whole people never
were *encouraged*, now or at any time; they are always
provoked?"

When all these things have been noted, to hold a man
to his formulæ without reference to their special application, is pure pedantry. Burke was the last man to lay
down any political proposition not subject to the ever va-
rying interpretation of circumstances, and independently of
the particular use which was to be made of it. Nothing
universal, he had always said, can be rationally affirmed on
any moral or political subject. The lines of morality,
again, are never ideal lines of mathematics, but are broad
and deep as well as long, admitting of exceptions, and de-
manding modifications. "These exceptions and modifications are made, not by the process of logic, but by the
rules of prudence. Prudence is not only first in rank of
the virtues, political and moral, but she is the director, the
regulator, the standard of them all. As no moral questions are ever abstract questions, this, before I judge upon
any abstract proposition, must be embodied in circumstances; for, since things are right and wrong, morally
speaking, only by their relation and connection with other
things, this very question of what it is politically right to
grant, depends upon its relation to its effects." "Circumstances," he says, never weary of laying down his great
notion of political method, "give, in reality, to every political principle its distinguishing colour and discriminat-
ing effect. The circumstances are what render every civil
and political scheme beneficial or obnoxious to mankind."

This is at once the weapon with which he would have
defended his own consistency, and attacked the absolute

proceedings in France.   He changed his front, but he
never changed his ground.   He was not more passionate
against the proscription in France than he had been against
the suspension of Habeas Corpus in the American war.   " I
flatter myself," he said in the *Reflections*, " that I love a
manly, moral, regulated liberty."   Ten years before he had
said, " The liberty, the only liberty I mean, is a liberty connected with order."   The court tried to regulate liberty
too severely.   It found in him an inflexible opponent.
Demagogues tried to remove the regulations of liberty.
They encountered in him the bitterest and most unceasing
of all remonstrants.   The arbitrary majority in the House
of Commons forgot for whose benefit they held power,
from whom they derived their authority, and in what description of government it was that they had a place.
Burke was the most valiant and strenuous champion in the
ranks of the independent minority.   He withstood to the
face the King and the King's friends.   He withstood to the
face Charles Fox and the Friends of the People.   He may
have been wrong in both, or in either, but it is unreasonable to tell us that he turned back in his course; that he
was a revolutionist in 1770, and a reactionist in 1790;
that he was in his sane mind when he opposed the supremacy of the Court, but that his reason was tottering when
he opposed the supremacy of the Faubourg Saint Antoine.

There is no part of Burke's career at which we may not
find evidence of his instinctive and undying repugnance to
the critical or revolutionary spirit and all its works.   From
the early days when he had parodied Bolingbroke, down
to the later time when he denounced Condorcet as a fanatical atheist, with "every disposition to the lowest as well
as the highest and most determined villanies," he invariably suspected or denounced everybody, virtuous or vicious,

high-minded or ignoble, who inquired with too keen a
scrutiny into the foundations of morals, of religion, of social order.   To examine with a curious or unfavourable eye
the bases of established opinions, was to show a leaning
to anarchy, to atheism, or to unbridled libertinism.   Already we have seen how, three years after the publication
of his *Thoughts on the Present Discontents*, and seventeen years before the composition of the *Reflections*, he
denounced the philosophers with a fervour and a vehemence which he never afterwards surpassed.   When some
of the clergy petitioned to be relieved from some of the
severities of subscription, he had resisted them on the bold
ground that the truth of a proposition deserves less attention than the effect of adherence to it upon the established
order of things.   "I will not enter into the question," he
told the House of Commons, "how much truth is prefera-
ble to peace.   Perhaps truth may be far better.   But as
we have scarcely ever the same certainty in the one that
we have in the other, I would, unless the truth were evi-
dent indeed, hold fast to peace."   In that intellectual rest-
lessness, to which the world is so deeply indebted, Burke
could recognize but scanty merit.   Himself the most industrious and active-minded of men, he was ever sober in
cutting the channels of his activity, and he would have
had others equally moderate.   Perceiving that plain and
righteous conduct is the end of life in this world, he
prayed men not to be over-curious in searching for, and
handling, and again handling, the theoretic base on which
the prerogatives of virtue repose.   Provided that there
was peace, that is to say, so much of fair happiness and
content as is compatible with the conditions of the human
lot, Burke felt that a too great inquisitiveness as to its
foundations was not only idle but cruel.

If the world continues to read the *Reflections*, and reads it with a new admiration that is not diminished by the fact that on the special issue its tendency is every day more clearly discerned to have been misleading, we may be sure that it is not for the sake of such things as the precise character of the Revolution of 1688, where, for that matter, constitutional writers have shown abundantly that Burke was nearly as much in the wrong as Dr. Sacheverell. Nor has the book lived merely by its gorgeous rhetoric and high emotions, though these have been contributing elements. It lives because it contains a sentiment, a method, a set of informal principles, which, awakened into new life after the Revolution, rapidly transformed the current ways of thinking and feeling about all the most serious objects of our attention, and have powerfully helped to give a richer substance to all modern literature. In the *Reflections* we have the first great sign that the ideas on government and philosophy which Locke had been the chief agent in setting into European circulation, and which had carried all triumphantly before them throughout the century, did not comprehend the whole truth nor the deepest truth about human character—the relations of men and the union of men in society. It has often been said that the armoury from which the French philosophers of the eighteenth century borrowed their weapons was furnished from England, and it may be added as truly that the reaction against that whole scheme of thought came from England. In one sense we may call the *Reflections* a political pamphlet, but it is much more than this, just as the movement against which it was levelled was much more than a political movement. The Revolution rested on a philosophy, and Burke confronted it with an antagonistic philosophy. Those are but superficial readers who fail to

8*

see at how many points Burke, while seeming only to deal
with the French monarchy and the British constitution,
with Dr. Price and Marie Antoinette, was in fact, and exactly because he dealt with them in the comprehensive
spirit of true philosophy, turning men's minds to an attitude from which not only the political incidents of the
hour, but the current ideas about religion, psychology, the
very nature of human knowledge, would all be seen in a
changed light and clothed in new colour. All really profound speculation about society comes in time to touch the
heart of every other object of speculation, not by directly
contributing new truths or directly corroborating old ones,
but by setting men to consider the consequences to life of
different opinions on these abstract subjects, and their relations to the great paramount interests of society, however
those interests may happen at the time to be conceived.
Burke's book marks a turning-point in literary history,
because it was the signal for that reaction over the whole
field of thought, into which the Revolution drove many of
the finest minds of the next generation, by showing the
supposed consequences of pure individualistic rationalism.

We need not attempt to work out the details of this ex-
tension of a political reaction into a universal reaction in
philosophy and poetry. Any one may easily think out
for himself what consequences in act and thought, as well
as in government, would be likely to flow, for example,
from one of the most permanently admirable sides of
Burke's teaching—his respect for the collective reason of
men, and his sense of the impossibility in politics and
morals of considering the individual apart from the experience of the race. " We are afraid," he says, " to put
men to live and trade each on his own private stock of
reason, because we suspect that this stock in each man is

small, and that the individuals would do better to avail
themselves of the general bank and capital of nations and
of ages. *Many of our men of speculation, instead of exploding general prejudices, employ their sagacity to discover the latent wisdom which prevails in them.* If they find
what they seek, and they seldom fail, they think it more
wise to continue the prejudice with the reason involved,
than to cast away the coat of prejudice, and to leave nothing but the naked reason : because prejudice with its reason has a motive to give action to that reason, and an affection which will give it permanence. Prejudice is of
ready application in the emergency ; it previously engages
the mind in a steady course of wisdom and virtue, and
does not leave the man hesitating in the moment of deci-
sion, sceptical, puzzled, and unresolved. Prejudice renders
a man's virtue his habit, and not a series of unconnected
acts. Through just prejudice, his duty becomes a part of his
nature." Is not this to say, in other words, that in every
man the substantial foundations of action consist of the
accumulated layers which various generations of ancestors
have placed for him ; that the greater part of our sentiments act most effectively when they act most mechanical-
ly, and by the methods of an unquestioned system ; that
although no rule of conduct or spring of action ought to
endure which does not repose in sound reason, yet this
naked reason is in itself a less effective means of influenc-
ing action than when it exists as one part of a fabric of
ancient and endeared association ? Interpreted by a mo-
bile genius and expanded by a poetic imagination, all this
became the foundation from which the philosophy of
Coleridge started, and, as Mill has shown in a famous essay, Coleridge was the great apostle of the conservative
spirit in England in its best form.

Though Burke here, no doubt, found a true base for the philosophy of order, yet perhaps Condorcet or Barnave might have justly asked him whether, when we thus realize the strong and immovable foundations which are laid in our character before we are born, there could be any occasion, as a matter of fact, for that vehement alarm which moved Burke lest a few lawyers, by a score of parchment decrees, should overthrow the venerated sentiments of Europe about justice and about property? Should he not have known better than most men the force of the self-protecting elements of society?

This is not a convenient place for discussing the issues between the school of order and the school of progress. It is enough to have marked Burke's position in one of them. The *Reflections* places him among the great Conservatives of history. Perhaps the only Englishman with whom in this respect he may be compared is Sir Thomas More, that virtuous and eloquent reactionist of the sixteenth century. More abounded in light, in intellectual interests, in single-minded care for the common weal. He was as anxious as any man of his time for the improved ordering of the Church, but he could not endure that reformation should be bought at the price of breaking up the ancient spiritual unity of Europe. He was willing to slay and be slain rather than he would tolerate the destruction of the old faith, or assent to the violence of the new statecraft. He viewed Thomas Cromwell's policy of reformation just as Burke viewed Mirabeau's policy of revolution. Burke too, we may be very sure, would as willingly have sent Mirabeau and Bailly to prison or the block as More sent Phillips to the Tower and Bainham to the stake. For neither More nor Burke was of the gentle contemplative spirit, which the first disorder of a new so-

ciety just bursting into life merely overshadows with sad-
dening regrets and poetic gloom. The old harmony was
to them so bound up with the purpose and meaning of
life, that to wage active battle for the gods of their reverence was the irresistible instinct of self-preservation. More
had an excuse which Burke had not, for the principle of
persecution was accepted by the best minds of the sixteenth century, but by the best minds of the eighteenth it
was emphatically repudiated.

Another illustrious name of Burke's own era rises to
our lips, as we ponder mentally the too scanty list of those
who have essayed the great and hardy task of reconciling
order with progress. Turgot is even a more imposing
figure than Burke himself. The impression made upon
us by the pair is indeed very different, for Turgot was
austere, reserved, distant, a man of many silences, and
much suspense; while Burke, as we know, was imaginative, exuberant, unrestrained, and, like some of the greatest actors on the stage of human affairs, he had associated
his own personality with the prevalence of right ideas and
good influences. In Turgot, on the other hand, we discern something of the isolation, the sternness, the disdain-
ful melancholy of Tacitus. He even rises out of the eager,
bustling, shrill-tongued crowd of the Voltairean age with
some of that austere moral indignation and haughty astonishment with which Dante had watched the stubborn
ways of men centuries before. On one side Turgot shared
the conservatism of Burke, though, perhaps, he would
hardly have given it that name. He habitually corrected
the headlong insistence of the revolutionary philosophers,
his friends, by reminding them that neither pity, nor benevolence, nor hope can ever dispense with justice; and
he could never endure to hear of great changes being

wrought at the cost of this sovereign quality. Like Burke,
he held fast to the doctrine that everything must be done
for the multitude, but nothing by them. Like Burke, he
realized how close are the links that bind the successive
generations of men, and make up the long chain of human
history. Like Burke, he never believed that the human
mind has any spontaneous inclination to welcome pure
truth. Here, however, is visible between them a hard line
of division. It is not error, said Turgot, which opposes
the progress of truth; it is indolence, obstinacy, and the
spirit of routine. But then Turgot enjoined upon us to
make it the aim of life to do battle in ourselves and others
with all this indolence, obstinacy, and spirit of routine in
the world; while Burke, on the contrary, gave to these
bad things gentler names, he surrounded them with the
picturesque associations of the past, and in the great world-
crisis of his time he threw all his passion and all his genius
on their side. Will any reader doubt which of these two
types of the school of order and justice, both of them noble, is the more valuable for the race, and the worthier and
more stimulating ideal for the individual?

It is not certain that Burke was not sometimes for a
moment startled by the suspicion that he might unawares
be fighting against the truth. In the midst of flaming
and bitter pages, we now and again feel a cool breath from
the distant region of a half-pensive tolerance. "I do not
think," he says at the close of the *Reflections*, to the person to whom they were addressed, "that my sentiments
are likely to alter yours. I do not know that they ought.
You are young; you cannot guide, but must follow, the
fortune of your country. But hereafter they may be of
some use to you, in some future form which your commonwealth may take. In the present it can hardly re-

VIII.]   TURGOT.   175

main; but before its final settlement, it may be obliged to pass, as one of our poets says, 'through great varieties of untried being,' and in all its transmigrations to be purified by fire and blood."

He felt in the midst of his hate that what he took for seething chaos might after all be the struggle upwards of the germs of order. Among the later words that he wrote on the Revolution were these: "If a great change is to be made in human affairs, the minds of men will be fitted to it; the general opinions and feelings will draw that way. Every fear, every hope, will forward it; and then they who persist in opposing this mighty current in human affairs will appear rather to resist the decrees of Providence itself than the mere designs of men." We can only regret that these rays of the *mens divinior* did not shine with a more steadfast light; and that a spirit which, amid the sharp press of manifold cares and distractions, had ever vibrated with lofty sympathies, was not now more constant to its faith in the beneficent powers and processes of the Unseen Time.

CHAPTER IX.

For some months after the publication of the *Reflections*,
Burke kept up the relations of an armed peace with his
old political friends. The impeachment went on, and in
December (1790) there was a private meeting on the business connected with it, between Pitt, Burke, Fox, and Dun-
das, at the house of the Speaker. It was described by one
who knew as most snug and amiable, and there seems to
have been a general impression in the world at this moment that Fox might by some means be induced to join
Pitt. What troubled the slumbers of good Whigs like
Gilbert Elliot was the prospect of Fox committing himself
too strongly on French affairs. Burke himself was in the
deepest dejection at the prospect; for Fox did not cease
to express the most unqualified disapproval of the *Reflections;* he thought that, even in point of composition, it
was the worst thing that Burke had ever published. It
was already feared that his friendship for Sheridan was
drawing him further away from Burke, with whom Sheridan had quarrelled, into a course of politics that would
both damage his own reputation, and break up the strong
union of which the Duke of Portland was the nominal
head.

New floods in France had not yet carried back the ship

of state into raging waters. Pitt was thinking so little of
danger from that country, that he had plunged into a policy of intervention in the affairs of eastern Europe. When
writers charge Burke with breaking violently in upon Pitt's
system of peace abroad and reform at home, they overlook
the fact that before Burke had begun to preach his crusade against the Jacobins, Pitt had already prepared a war
with Russia. The nation refused to follow. They agreed
with Fox that it was no concern of theirs whether or not
Russia took from Turkey the country between the Boug
and Dniester; they felt that British interests would be
more damaged by the expenses of a war than by the acquisition by Russia of Ockzakow. Pitt was obliged to
throw up the scheme, and to extricate himself as well as
he could from rash engagements with Prussia. It was on
account of his services to the cause of peace on this occasion that Catharine ordered the Russian ambassador to
send her a bust of Fox in white marble, to be placed in
her colonnade between Demosthenes and Cicero. We may
take it for granted that after the Revolution rose to its full
height, the bust of Fox accompanied that of Voltaire down
to the cellar of the Hermitage.

While the affair of the Russian armament was still oc-
cupying the minister, an event of signal importance happened in the ranks of his political adversaries. The alliance which had lasted between Burke and Fox for five-and-
twenty years came to a sudden end, and this rift gradually widened into a destructive breach throughout the party.
There is no parallel in our parliamentary history to the
fatal scene. In Ireland, indeed, only eight years before,
Flood and Grattan, after fighting side by side for many
years, had all at once sprung upon one another in the
Parliament House with the fury of vultures : Flood had

screamed to Grattan that he was a mendicant patriot, and
Grattan had called Flood an ill-omened bird of night, with
a sepulchral note, a cadaverous aspect, and a broken beak.
The Irish, like the French, have the art of making things
dramatic, and Burke was the greatest of Irishmen.   On
the opening of the session of 1791, the government had
introduced a bill for the better government of Canada.   It
introduced questions about church establishments and hereditary legislators.   In discussing these, Fox made some
references to France.   It was impossible to refer to France
without touching the *Reflections on the French Revolution.*
Burke was not present, but he heard what Fox had said,
and before long Fox again introduced French affairs in a
debate on the Russian armament.   Burke rose in violent
heat of mind to reply, but the House would not hear him.
He resolved to speak when the time came for the Canada
Bill to be recommitted.   Meanwhile some of his friends
did all that they could to dissuade him from pressing the
matter further.   Even the Prince of Wales is said to have
written him a letter.   There were many signs of the rupture that was so soon to come in the Whig ranks.   Men
so equally devoted to the common cause as Windham and
Elliot nearly came to a quarrel at a dinner-party at Lord
Malmesbury's, on the subject of Burke's design to speak;
and Windham, who for the present sided with Fox, enters
in his diary that he was glad to escape from the room
without speaking to the man whom, since the death of
Dr. Johnson, he revered before all others.

On the day appointed for the Canada Bill, Fox called at
Burke's house, and after some talk on Burke's intention to
speak, and on other matters, they walked down to Westminster and entered the House together, as they had so
many a time done before, but were never to do again.

They found that the debate had been adjourned, and it was not until May 6th that Burke had an opportunity of explaining himself on the Revolution in France. He had no sooner risen, than interruptions broke out from his own side, and a scene of great disorder followed. Burke was incensed beyond endurance by this treatment, for even Fox and Windham had taken part in the tumult against him. With much bitterness he commented on Fox's previous eulogies of the Revolution, and finally there came the fatal words of severance. "It is indiscreet," he said, "at any period, but especially at my time of life, to provoke enemies, or give my friends occasion to desert me. Yet if my firm and steady adherence to the British Constitution place me in such a dilemma, I am ready to risk it, and with my last words to exclaim, 'Fly from the French Constitution.'" Fox at this point eagerly called to him that there was no loss of friends. "Yes, yes," cried Burke, "there is a loss of friends. I know the price of my conduct. I have done my duty at the price of my friend. Our friendship is at an end."

The members who sat on the same side were aghast at proceedings which went beyond their worst apprehensions. Even the ministerialists were shocked. Pitt agreed much more with Fox than with Burke, but he would have been more than human if he had not watched with complacency his two most formidable adversaries turning their swords against one another. Wilberforce, who was more disinterested, lamented the spectacle as shameful. In the galleries there was hardly a dry eye. Fox, as might have been expected from his warm and generous nature, was deeply moved, and is described as weeping even to sobbing. He repeated his former acknowledgment of his debt to Burke, and he repeated his former expression of

faith in the blessings which the abolition of royal despotism would bring to France. With unabated vehemence
Burke again rose to denounce the French Constitution—
"a building composed of untempered mortar—the work
of Goths and Vandals, where everything was disjointed
and inverted." After a short rejoinder from Fox, the
scene came to a close, and the once friendly intercourse
between the two heroes was at an end. When they met
in the Managers' box in Westminster Hall on the business
of Hastings's trial, they met with the formalities of stran-
gers. There is a story that when Burke left the House
on the night of the quarrel it was raining, and Mr. Curwen, a member of the Opposition, took him home in his
carriage. Burke at once began to declaim against the
French. Curwen dropped some remark on the other side.
"What!" Burke cried out, grasping the check-string, "are
you one of these people! Set me down." It needed all
Curwen's force to keep him where he was; and when they
reached his house, Burke stepped out without saying a
single word.

We may agree that all this did not indicate the perfect
sobriety and self-control proper to a statesman, in what
was a serious crisis both to his party and to Europe. It
was about this time that Burke said to Addington, who
was then Speaker of the House of Commons, that he was
not well. "I eat too much, Speaker," he said, "I drink
too much, and I sleep too little." It is even said that he
felt the final breach with Fox as a relief from unendurable
suspense; and he quoted the lines about Æneas, after he
had finally resolved to quit Dido and the Carthaginian
shore, at last being able to snatch slumber in his ship's tall
stern. There can be no doubt how severe had been the
tension. Yet the performance to which Burke now ap-

plied himself is one of the gravest and most reasonable of all his compositions. He felt it necessary to vindicate the fundamental consistency between his present and his past. We have no difficulty in imagining the abuse to which he was exposed from those whose abuse gave him pain. In a country governed by party, a politician who quits the allies of a lifetime must expect to pay the penalty. The Whig papers told him that he was expected to surrender his seat in Parliament. They imputed to him all sorts of sinister motives. His name was introduced into ironical toasts. For a whole year there was scarcely a member of his former party who did not stand aloof from him. Windham, when the feeling was at its height, sent word to a host that he would rather not meet Burke at dinner. Dr. Parr, though he thought Mr. Burke the greatest man upon earth, declared himself most indignantly and most fixedly on the side of Mr. Sheridan and Mr. Fox. The Duke of Portland, though always described as strongly and fondly attached to him, and Gilbert Elliot, who thought that Burke was right in his views on the Revolution, and right in expressing them, still could not forgive the open catastrophe, and for many months all the old habits of intimacy among them were entirely broken off.

Burke did not bend to the storm. He went down to Margate, and there finished the *Appeal from the New to the Old Whigs*. Meanwhile he dispatched his son to Coblenz to give advice to the royalist exiles, who were then mainly in the hands of Calonne, one of the very worst of the ministers whom Louis XVI. had tried between his dismissal of Turgot in 1774, and the meeting of the States-General in 1789. This measure was taken at the request of Calonne, who had visited Burke at Margate. The English government did not disapprove of it, though they naturally declined to invest either young Burke or any one else with authority from themselves. As little came of the mission as might have been expected from the frivolous, unmanly, and enraged spirit of those to whom it was addressed.

In August (1791), while Richard Burke was at Coblenz, the *Appeal* was published. This was the last piece that Burke wrote on the Revolution, in which there is any pretence of measure, sobriety, and calm judgment in face of a formidable and perplexing crisis. Henceforth it is not political philosophy, but the minatory exhortation of a prophet. We deal no longer with principles and ideas, but with a partisan denunciation of particular acts, and a partisan incitement to a given practical policy. We may appreciate the policy as we choose, but our appreciation of Burke as a thinker and a contributor to political wisdom is at an end. He is now only Demosthenes thundering against Philip, or Cicero shrieking against Mark Antony.

The *Reflections* had not been published many months before Burke wrote the *Letter to a Member of the National Assembly* (January, 1791), in which strong disapproval had grown into furious hatred. It contains the elaborate diatribe against Rousseau, the grave panegyric on Cromwell for choosing Hale to be Chief Justice, and a sound criticism on the laxity and want of foresight in the manner in which the States-General had been convened. Here first Burke advanced to the position that it might be the duty of other nations to interfere to restore the King to his rightful authority, just as England and Prussia had interfered to save Holland from confusion, as they had interfered to preserve the hereditary constitution in the Austrian Netherlands, and as Prussia had interfered to snatch even the malignant and the turban'd Turk from the pounce

of the Russian eagle. Was not the King of France as
much an object of policy and compassion as the Grand
Seignior? As this was the first piece in which Burke
hinted at a crusade, so it was the first in which he began
to heap upon the heads, not of Hébert, Fouquier-Tinville,
Billaud, nor even of Robespierre or Danton—for none of
these had yet been heard of—but of able and conscientious men in the Constituent Assembly, language of a
virulence which Fox once said seriously that Burke had
picked, even to the phrases of it, out of the writings of
Salmasius against Milton, but which is really only to be
paralleled by the much worse language of Milton against
Salmasius. It was in truth exactly the kind of incensed
speech which, at a later date, the factions in Paris levelled against one another, when Girondins screamed for the
heads of Jacobins, and Robespierre denounced Danton,
and Tallien cried for the blood of Robespierre.

Burke declined most wisely to suggest any plan for the
National Assembly. "Permit me to say"—this is in the
letter of January, 1791, to a member of the Assembly—
"that if I were as confident as I ought to be diffident in
my own loose general ideas, I never should venture to
broach them, if but at twenty leagues' distance from the
centre of your affairs. I must see with my own eyes; I
must in a manner touch with my own hands, not only the
fixed, but momentary circumstances, before I could venture
to suggest any political project whatsoever. I must know
the power and disposition to accept, to execute, to perse-
vere. I must see all the aids and all the obstacles. I
must see the means of correcting the plan, where correc-
tives would be wanted. I must see the things: I must
see the men. Without a concurrence and adaptation of
these to the design, the very best speculative projects

might become not only useless but mischievous. Plans
must be made for men. People at a distance must judge
ill of men. They do not always answer to their reputation when you approach them. Nay, the perspective va-
ries, and shows them quite other than you thought them.
At a distance, if we judge uncertainly of men, we must
judge worse of *opportunities*, which continually vary their
shapes and colours, and pass away like clouds." Our admiration at such words is quickly stifled when we recall
the confident, unsparing, immoderate criticism which both
preceded and followed this truly rational exposition of the
danger of advising, in cases where we know neither the
men nor the opportunities. Why was savage and unfal-
tering denunciation any less unbecoming than, as he admits, crude prescriptions would have been unbecoming?

By the end of 1791, when he wrote the *Thoughts on
French Affairs*, he had penetrated still further into the es-
sential character of the Revolution. Any notion of a reform to be effected after the decorous pattern of 1688, so
conspicuous in the first great manifesto, had wholly disappeared. The changes in France he allowed to bear little
resemblance or analogy to any of those which had been
previously brought about in Europe. It is a revolution,
he said, of doctrine and theoretic dogma. The Reformation was the last revolution of this sort which had happened in Europe; and he immediately goes on to remark a
point of striking resemblance between them. The effect
of the Reformation was "to introduce other interests into
all countries than those which arose from their locality
and natural circumstances." In like manner other sources
of faction were now opened, combining parties among the
inhabitants of different countries into a single connection.
From these sources, effects were likely to arise fully as im-

portant as those which had formerly arisen from the jar-
ring interests of the religious sects.   It is a species of faction which " breaks the locality of public affections."[1]

He was thus launched on the full tide of his policy.
The French Revolution must be hemmed in by a cordon
of fire.   Those who sympathised with it in England must
be gagged, and if gagging did not suffice, they must be
taught respect for the constitution in dungeons and on the
gallows.   His cry for war abroad and arbitrary tyranny at
home waxed louder every day.   As Fox said, it was lucky
that Burke took the royal side in the Revolution, for his
violence would certainly have got him hanged if he had
happened to take the other side.

It was in the early summer of 1792 that Miss Burney
again met Burke at Mrs. Crewe's villa at Hampstead.   He
entered into an animated conversation on Lord Macartney
and the Chinese expedition, reviving all the old enthusiasm
of his companion by his allusions and anecdotes, his brilliant fancies and wide information.   When politics were
introduced, he spoke with an eagerness and a vehemence
that instantly banished the graces, though it redoubled the
energies of his discourse.   " How I wish," Miss Burney
writes, " that you could meet this wonderful man when he
is easy, happy, and with people he cordially likes.   But
politics, even on his own side, must always be excluded;

---

[1] De Tocqueville has unconsciously imitated Burke's very phrases.
" Toutes les révolutions civiles et politiques ont eu une patrie, et s'y
sont enfermées.   La Révolution française . . . on l'a vue rapprocher
ou diviser les hommes en dépit des lois, des traditions, des caractères,
de langue, rendant parfois ennemis des compatriotes, et frères des
étrangers; *ou plutôt elle a formé audessus de toutes les nationalités par-
ticulières, une patrie intellectuelle commune dont les hommes de toutes les
nations ont pu devenir citoyens.*"—Ancien Régime, p. 15.

his irritability is so terrible on that theme, that it gives immediately to his face *the expression of a man who is going to defend himself from murderers.*"

Burke still remained without a following, but the ranks of his old allies gradually began to show signs of wavering. His panic about the Jacobins within the gates slowly spread. His old faith, about which he had once talked so much, in the ancient rustic, manly, home-bred sense of the English people, he dismissed as if it had been some idle dream that had come to him through the ivory gate. His fine comparison of the nation to a majestic herd, browsing in peace amid the importunate chirrupings of a thousand crickets, became so little appropriate, that he was now beside himself with apprehension that the crickets were about to rend the oxen in pieces. Even then the herd stood tranquilly in their pastures, only occasionally turning a dull eye, now to France, and now to Burke. In the autumn of 1791, Burke dined with Pitt and Lord Grenville, and he found them resolute for an honest neutrality in the affairs of France, and " quite out of all apprehensions of any effect from the French Revolution in this kingdom, either at present or any time to come." Francis and Sheridan, it is true, spoke as if they almost wished for a domestic convulsion; and cool observers who saw him daily, even accused Sheridan of wishing to stir up the lower ranks of the people by the hope of plundering their betters. But men who afterwards became alarmists are found, so late as the spring of 1792, declaring in their most confidential correspondence that the party of confusion made no way with the country, and produced no effect. Horne Tooke was its most conspicuous chief, and nobody pretended to fear the subversion of the realm by Horne Tooke. Yet Burke, in letters where he admits that

the democratic party is entirely discountenanced, and that
the Jacobin faction in England is under a heavy cloud,
was so possessed by the spectre of panic, as to declare
that the Duke of Brunswick was as much fighting the
battle of the crown of England as the Duke of Cumber-
land fought that battle at Culloden.

Time and events, meanwhile, had been powerfully telling for Burke. While he was writing his *Appeal*, the
French King and Queen had destroyed whatever confidence sanguine dreamers might have had in their loyalty
to the new order of things, by attempting to escape over
the frontier. They were brought back, and a manful attempt was made to get the new constitution to work, in
the winter of 1791–92. It was soon found out that
Mirabeau had been right, when he said that for a monarchy it was too democratic, and for a republic there was
a king too much. This was Burke's *Reflections* in a nut-
shell. But it was foreign intervention that finally ruined
the King, and destroyed the hope of an orderly issue.
Frederick the Great had set the first example of what
some call iniquity and violence in Europe, and others in
milder terms call a readjustment of the equilibrium of
nations. He had taken Silesia from the House of Austria, and he had shared in the first partition of Poland.
Catharine II. had followed him at the expense of Poland,
Sweden, and Turkey. However we may view these transactions, and whether we describe them by the stern words
of the moralist, or the more deprecatory words of the
diplomatist, they are the first sources of that storm of law-
less rapine which swept over every part of Europe for five-
and-twenty years to come. The intervention of Austria
and Prussia in the affairs of France was originally less a
deliberate design for the benefit of the old order than an

interlude in the intrigues of eastern Europe. But the first
effect of intervention on behalf of the French monarchy
was to bring it in a few weeks to the ground.

In the spring of 1792 France replied to the preparations of Austria and Prussia for invasion by a declaration
of war. It was inevitable that the French people should
associate the court with the foreign enemy that was coming to its deliverance. Everybody knew as well then as
we know it now, that the Queen was as bitterly incensed
against the new order of things, and as resolutely unfaith-
ful to it, as the most furious emigrant on the Rhine. Even
Burke himself, writing to his son at Coblenz, was con-
strained to talk about Marie Antoinette as that " most unfortunate woman, who was not to be cured of the spirit of
court intrigue even by a prison." The King may have
been loyally resigned to his position, but resignation will
not defend a country from the invader; and the nation
distrusted a chief who only a few months before had been
arrested in full flight to join the national enemy. Power
naturally fell into the hands of the men of conviction, energy, passion, and resource. Patriotism and republicanism
became synonymous, and the constitution against which
Burke had prophesied was henceforth a dead letter. The
spirit of insurrection that had slumbered since the fall
of the Bastille and the march to Versailles in 1789, now
awoke in formidable violence, and after the preliminary re-
hearsal of what is known in the revolutionary calendar as
the 20th of June (1792), the people of Paris responded to
the Duke of Brunswick's insensate manifesto by the more
memorable day of the 10th of August. Brunswick, ac-
cepting the hateful language which the French emigrants
put into his mouth, had declared that every member of the
national guard taken with arms in his hands would be im-

mediately put to death; that every inhabitant who should dare to defend himself, would be put to death and his house burnt to the ground; and that if the least insult was offered to the royal family, then their Austrian and Prussian majesties would deliver Paris to military execution and total destruction. This is the vindictive ferocity which only civil war can kindle. To convince men that the manifesto was not an empty threat, on the day of its publication a force of nearly 140,000 Austrians, Prussians, and Hessians entered France. The sections of Paris replied by marching to the Tuileries, and after a furious conflict with the Swiss guards, they stormed the chateau. The King and his family had fled to the National Assembly. The same evening they were thrown into prison, whence the King and Queen only came out on their way to the scaffold.

It was the King's execution in January, 1793, that finally raised feeling in England to the intense heat which Burke had for so long been craving. The evening on which the courier brought the news was never forgotten by those who were in London at the time. The playhouses were instantly closed, and the audiences insisted on retiring with half the amusement for which they had paid. People of the lowest and the highest rank alike put on mourning. The French were universally denounced as fiends upon earth. It was hardly safe for a Frenchman to appear in the streets of London. Placards were posted on every wall, calling for war, and the crowds who gathered round them read them with loud hurrahs.

It would be a great mistake to say that Pitt ever lost his head, but he lost his feet. The momentary passion of the nation forced him out of the pacific path in which he

would have chosen to stay. Burke had become the greatest power in the country, and was in closer communication
with the ministers than any one out of office. He went
once about this time with Windham and Elliot, to inform
Pitt as to the uneasiness of the public about the slackness
of our naval and military preparation. "Burke," says one
of the party, "gave Pitt a little political instruction in a
very respectful and cordial way, but with the authority of
an old and most informed statesman, and although nobody
ever takes the whole of Burke's advice, yet he often, or always rather, furnishes very important and useful matter,
some part of which sticks and does good. Pitt took it all
very patiently and cordially."

It was in the December of 1792 that Burke had enacted
that famous bit of melodrama out of place, known as the
Dagger Scene. The Government had brought in an Alien
Bill, imposing certain pains and restrictions on foreigners
coming to this country. Fox denounced it as a concession
to foolish alarms, and was followed by Burke, who began
to storm as usual against murderous atheists. Then, without due preparation, he began to fumble in his bosom, suddenly drew out a dagger, and with an extravagant gesture
threw it on the floor of the House, crying that this was
what they had to expect from their alliance with France.
The stroke missed its mark, and there was a general inclination to titter, until Burke, collecting himself for an effort, called upon them with a vehemence to which his lis-
teners could not choose but respond, to keep French principles from their heads, and French daggers from their
hearts; to preserve all their blandishments in life, and all
their consolations in death; all the blessings of time, and
all the hopes of eternity. All this was not prepared long
beforehand, for it seems that the dagger had only been

shown to Burke on his way to the House, as one that had been sent to Birmingham to be a pattern for a large order. Whether prepared or unprepared, the scene was one from which we gladly avert our eyes.

Negotiations had been going on for some months, and they continued in various stages for some months longer, for a coalition between the two great parties of the state. Burke was persistently anxious that Fox should join Pitt's government. Pitt always admitted the importance of Fox's abilities in the difficult affairs which lay before the ministry, and declared that he had no sort of personal animosity to Fox, but rather a personal good-will and good-liking. Fox himself said of a coalition, "It is so damned right, to be sure, that I cannot help thinking it must be." But the difficulties were insuperable. The more rapidly the government drifted in Burke's direction, the more impossible was it for a man of Fox's political sympathies and convictions to have any dealings with a cabinet committed to a policy of irrational panic, to be carried out by a costly war abroad and cruel repression at home. "*What a very wretched man!*" was Burke's angry exclamation one day, when it became certain that Fox meant to stand by the old flag of freedom and generous common-sense.

When the coalition at length took place (1794), the only man who carried Burke's principles to their fullest extent into Pitt's cabinet was Windham. It is impossible not to feel the attraction of Windham's character, his amiability, his reverence for great and virtuous men, his passion for knowledge, the versatility of his interests. He is a striking example of the fact that literature was a common pursuit and occupation to the chief statesmen of that time (always excepting Pitt), to an extent that has been gradually tending to become rarer. Windham, in the

midst of his devotion to public affairs, to the business of
his country, and, let us add, a zealous attendance on every
prize-fight within reach, was never happy unless he was
working up points in literature and mathematics.   There
was a literary and classical spirit abroad, and in spite of
the furious preoccupations of faction a certain ready dis-
engagement of mind prevailed.   If Windham and Fox began to talk of horses, they seemed to fall naturally into
what had been said about horses by the old writers.   Fox
held that long ears were a merit, and Windham met him
by the authority of Xenophon and Oppian in favour of
short ones, and finally they went off into what it was that
Virgil meant, when he called a horse's head *argutum
caput*.   Burke and Windham travelled in Scotland together in 1785, and their conversation fell as often on old
books as on Hastings or on Pitt.   They discussed Virgil's
similes; Johnson and L'Estrange, as the extremes of English style; what Stephens and A. Gellius had to say about
Cicero's use of the word *gratiosus*.   If they came to li-
braries, Windham ran into them with eagerness, and very
strongly enjoyed all " the *feel* that a library usually ex-
cites."   He is constantly reproaching himself with a re-
missness, which was purely imaginary, in keeping up his
mathematics, his Greek tragedies, his Latin historians.
There is no more curious example of the remorse of a
bookman impeded by affairs.   " What progress might
men make in the several parts of knowledge," he says very
truly, in one of these moods, " if they could only pursue
them with the same eagerness and assiduity as are exerted
by lawyers in the conduct of a suit."   But this distrac-
tion between the tastes of the bookman and the pursuits
of public business, united with a certain quality of his
constitution to produce one great defect in his character,

and it was the worst defect that a statesman can have.
He became the most irresolute and vacillating of men.
He wastes the first half of a day in deciding which of two
courses to take, and the second half in blaming himself
for not having taken the other.   He is constantly late at
entertainments, because he cannot make up his mind in
proper time whether to go or to stay at home; hesitation
whether he shall read in the red room or in the library,
loses him three of the best hours of a morning; the difficulty of early rising he finds to consist less in rising early,
than in satisfying himself that the practice is wholesome;
his mind is torn for a whole forenoon in an absurd contest with himself, whether he ought to indulge a strong
wish to exercise his horse before dinner.   Every page of
his diary is a register of the symptoms of this unhappy
disease.   When the Revolution came, he was absolutely
forced by the iron necessity of the case, after certain per-
turbations, to go either with Fox or with Burke.   Under
this compulsion he took one headlong plunge into the
policy of alarm.   Everybody knows how desperately an
habitually irresolute man is capable of clinging to a policy
or a conviction to which he has once been driven by dire
stress of circumstance.   Windham having at last made up
his mind to be frightened by the Revolution, was more
violently and inconsolably frightened than anybody else.

Pitt, after he had been forced into war, at least intended it to be a war on the good old-fashioned principles of
seizing the enemy's colonies and keeping them.   He was
taunted by the alarmists with caring only for sugar islands, and making himself master of all the islands in the
world except Great Britain and Ireland.   To Burke all
this was an abomination, and Windham followed Burke to
the letter.   He even declared the holy rage of the *Fourth*

9*

Letter on a Regicide Peace, published after Burke's death,
to contain the purest wisdom and the most unanswerable
policy. It was through Windham's eloquence and perseverance that the monstrous idea of a crusade, and all
Burke's other violent and excited precepts, gained an effective place and hearing in the cabinet, in the royal closet,
and in the House of Commons, long after Burke himself
had left the scene.

We have already seen how important an element Irish
affairs became in the war with America.   The same spirit
which had been stirred by the American war was inevitably kindled in Ireland by the French Revolution.   The
association of United Irishmen now came into existence,
with aims avowedly revolutionary.   They joined the party
which was striving for the relief of the Catholics from
certain disabilities, and for their admission to the franchise.
Burke had watched all movements in his native country,
from the Whiteboy insurrection of 1761 downwards, with
steady vigilance, and he watched the new movement of
1792 with the keenest eyes.   It made him profoundly
uneasy.   He could not endure the thought of ever so momentary and indirect an association with a revolutionary
party, either in Ireland or any other quarter of the globe,
yet he was eager for a policy which should reconcile the
Irish.   He was so for two reasons.   One of them was his
political sense of the inexpediency of proscribing men by
whole nations, and excluding from the franchise on the
ground of religion a people as numerous as the subjects of
the King of Denmark or the King of Sardinia, equal to
the population of the United Netherlands, and larger than
were to be found in all the States of Switzerland.   His
second reason was his sense of the urgency of facing trouble abroad with a nation united and contented at home ;

of abolishing in the heart of the country that "bank of discontent, every hour accumulating, upon which every description of seditious men may draw at pleasure."

In the beginning of 1792, Burke's son went to Dublin as the agent and adviser of the Catholic Committee, who at first listened to him with the respect due to one in whom they expected to find the qualities of his father. They soon found out that he was utterly without either tact or judgment; that he was arrogant, impertinent, vain, and empty. Wolfe Tone declared him to be by far the most impudent and opinionative fellow that he had ever known in his life. Nothing could exceed the absurdity of his conduct, and on one occasion he had a very narrow escape of being taken into custody by the Serjeant-at-arms, for rushing down from the gallery into the Irish House of Commons, and attempting to make a speech in defence of a petition which he had drawn up, and which was being attacked by a member in his place. Richard Burke went home, it is said, with two thousand guineas in his pocket, which the Catholics had cheerfully paid as the price of getting rid of him. He returned shortly after, but only helped to plunge the business into further confusion, and finally left the scene covered with odium and discredit. His father's *Letter to Sir Hercules Langrishe* (1792) remains an admirable monument of wise statesmanship, a singular interlude of calm and solid reasoning in the midst of a fiery whirlwind of intense passion. Burke perhaps felt that the state of Ireland was passing away from the sphere of calm and solid reason, when he knew that Dumouriez's victory over the allies at Valmy, which filled Beaconsfield with such gloom and dismay, was celebrated at Dublin by an illumination.

Burke, who was now in his sixty-fourth year, had for

some time announced his intention of leaving the House
of Commons, as soon as he had brought to an end the
prosecution of Hastings. In 1794 the trial came to a
close; the thanks of the House were formally voted to
the managers of the impeachment; and when the scene
was over, Burke applied for the Chiltern Hundreds. Lord
Fitzwilliam nominated Richard Burke for the seat which
his father had thus vacated at Malton. Pitt was then
making arrangements for the accession of the Portland
Whigs to his government, and it was natural, in connexion
with these arrangements, to confer some favour on the
man who had done more than anybody else to promote
the new alliance. It was proposed to make Burke a peer
under the style of Lord Beaconsfield — a title in a later
age whimsically borrowed for himself by a man of genius,
who delighted in irony. To the title it was proposed to
attach a yearly income for two or more lives. But the
bolt of destiny was at this instant launched. Richard
Burke, the adored centre of all his father's hopes and affections, was seized with illness, and died (August, 1794).
We cannot look without tragic emotion on the pathos of
the scene, which left the remnant of the old man's days
desolate and void. A Roman poet has described in touching words the woe of the aged Nestor, as he beheld the
funeral pile of his son, too untimely slain—

> " Oro parumper
> Attendas quantum de legibus ipse queratur
> Fatorum et nimio de stamine, quum videt acris
> Antilochi barbam ardentem : quum quærit ab omni
> Quisquis adest socius, cur hæc in tempora duret,
> Quod facinus dignum tam longo admiserit ævo."

Burke's grief finds a nobler expression. "The storm has
gone over me, and I lie like one of those old oaks which

the late hurricane has scattered about me. I am stripped
of all my honours; I am torn up by the roots and lie prostrate on the earth. . . . I am alone. I have none to meet
my enemies in the gate. . . . I live in an inverted order.
They who ought to have succeeded me have gone before
me. They who should have been to me as posterity, are
in the place of ancestors."

Burke only lived three years after this desolating blow.
The arrangements for a peerage, as a matter of course,
came to an end. But Pitt was well aware of the serious
embarrassments by which Burke was so pressed that he
saw actual beggary very close at hand. The King, too—
who had once, by the way, granted a pension to Burke's
detested Rousseau, though Rousseau was too proud to
draw it — seems to have been honourably interested in
making a provision for Burke. What Pitt offered was an
immediate grant of 1200*l*. a year from the Civil List for
Mrs. Burke's life, to be followed by a proposition to Parliament in a message from the King, to confer an annui-
ty of greater value upon a statesman who had served the
country to his own loss for thirty years. As a matter of
fact, the grant, 2500*l*. a year in amount, much to Burke's
chagrin, was never brought before Parliament, but was conferred directly by the Crown, as a charge on a certain stock
known as the West India four-and-a-half per cents. It
seems as if Pitt were afraid of challenging the opinion of
Parliament; and the storm which the pension raised out
of doors, was a measure of the trouble which the defence
of it would have inflicted on the government inside the
House of Commons. According to the rumour of the
time, Burke sold two of his pensions upon lives for
27,000*l*., and there was left the third pension of 1200*l*.
for his wife's life. By and by, when the resentment of

the Opposition was roused to the highest pitch by the infamous Treason and Sedition Bills of 1795, the Duke of Bedford and Lord Lauderdale, seeking to accumulate every possible complaint against the government, assailed the grant to Burke, as made without the consent of Parliament, and as a violent contradiction to the whole policy of the plan for economic reform.   The attack, if not unjustifiable in itself, came from an unlucky quarter.   A chief of the house of Bedford was the most unfit person in the world to protest against grants by favour of the Crown. Burke was too practised a rhetorician not to see the opening, and his *Letter to a Noble Lord* is the most splendid repartee in the English language.

It is not surprising that Burke's defence should have provoked rejoinder.   A cloud of pamphlets followed the *Letter to a Noble Lord*—some in doggrel verse, others in a magniloquent prose imitated from his own, others mere poisonous scurrility.   The nearest approach to a just stroke that I can find, after turning over a pile of this trash, is an expression of wonder that he, who was inconsolable for the loss of a beloved son, should not have reflected how many tender parents had been made childless in the profusion of blood, of which he himself had been the most relentless champion.   Our disgust at the pages of insult which were here levelled at a great man is perhaps moderated by the thought that Burke himself, who of all people ought to have known better, had held up to public scorn and obloquy men of such virtue, attainments, and real service to mankind as Richard Price and Joseph Priestley.

It was during these months that he composed the *Letters on a Regicide Peace*, though the third and fourth of them were not published until after his death.   There have been those to whom these compositions appeared to

be Burke's masterpieces.   In fact they are deplorable.
They contain passages of fine philosophy and of skilful
and plausible reasoning, but such passages only make us
wonder how they come to be where they are.   The reader
is in no humour for them.   In splendour of rhetoric, in
fine images, in sustention, in irony, they surpass anything
that Burke ever wrote ; but of the qualities and principles
that, far more than his rhetoric, have made Burke so admirable and so great—of justice, of firm grasp of fact, of
a reasonable sense of the probabilities of things—there are
only traces enough to light up the gulfs of empty words,
reckless phrases, and senseless vituperations, that surge and
boil around them.

It is with the same emotion of "grief and shame" with
which Fox heard Burke argue against relief to Dissenters,
that we hear him abusing the courts of law because they
did not convict Hardy and Horne Tooke.   The pages
against divorce and civil marriage, even granting that they
point to the right judgment in these matters, express it
with a vehemence that is irrational, and in the dialect, not
of a statesman, but of an enraged Capucin.   The highly-
wrought passage in which Burke describes external aggran-
disement as the original thought and the ultimate aim of
the earlier statesmen of the Revolution, is no better than
ingenious nonsense.   The whole performance rests on a
gross and inexcusable anachronism.   There is a contempt-
uous refusal to discriminate between groups of men who
were as different from one another as Oliver Cromwell was
different from James Nayler, and between periods which
were as unlike in all their conditions as the Athens of the
Thirty Tyrants was unlike Athens after Thrasybulus had
driven the Tyrants out.   He assumes that the men, the
policy, the maxims of the French government are the men,

the policy, and the maxims of the handful of obscure mis-
creants who had hacked priests and nobles to pieces at the
doors of the prisons four years before.   Carnot is to him
merely "that sanguinary tyrant," and the heroic Hoche
becomes "that old practised assassin," while the Prince of
Wales, by the way, and the Duke of York are the hope
and pride of nations.   To heap up that incessant iteration
about thieves, murderers, housebreakers, assassins, bandits,
bravoes with their hands dripping with blood and their
maw gorged with property, desperate paramours, bombas-
tical players, the refuse and rejected offal of strolling the-
atres, bloody buffoons, bloody felons—all this was as unjust to hundreds of disinterested, honest, and patriotic men
who were then earnestly striving to restore a true order
and solid citizenship in France, as the foul-mouthed scurrility of an Irish Orangeman is unjust to millions of de-
vout Catholics.

Burke was the man who might have been expected before all others to know that in every system of government, whatever may have been the crimes of its origin,
there is sure, by the bare necessity of things, to rise up a
party or an individual, whom their political instinct will
force into resistance to the fatalities of anarchy.   Man is
too strongly a political animal for it to be otherwise.   It
was so at each period and division in the Revolution.   There
was always a party of order; and by 1796, when Burke
penned these reckless philippics, order was only too easy
in France.   The Revolution had worn out the passion and
moral enthusiasm of its first years, and all the best men of
the revolutionary time had been consumed in a flame of
fire.   When Burke talked about this war being wholly unlike any war that ever was waged in Europe before, about
its being a war for justice on the one side, and a fanatical

bloody propagandism on the other, he shut his eyes to
the plain fact that the Directory had after all really sunk
to the moral level of Frederick and Catharine, or, for that
matter, of Louis the Fourteenth himself. This war was
only too like the other great wars of European history.
The French government had become political, exactly in
the same sense in which Thugut and Metternich and Herz-
berg were political. The French Republic in 1797 was
neither more nor less aggressive, immoral, piratical, than
the monarchies which had partitioned Poland, and had intended to redistribute the continent of Europe to suit their
own ambitions. The Coalition began the game, but France
proved too strong for them, and they had the worst of their
game. Jacobinism may have inspired the original fire which
made her armies irresistible, but Jacobinism of that stamp
had now gone out of fashion, and to denounce a peace with
the Directory because the origin of their government was
regicidal, was as childish as it would have been in Mazarin
to decline a treaty of regicide peace with Oliver Cromwell.

What makes the *Regicide Peace* so repulsive is not that
it recommends energetic prosecution of the war, and not
that it abounds in glaring fallacies in detail, but that it is
in direct contradiction with that strong, positive, rational, and sane method which had before uniformly marked
Burke's political philosophy. Here lay his inconsistency,
not in abandoning democratic principles, for he had never
held them, but in forgetting his own rules, that nations act
from adequate motives relative to their interests, and not
from metaphysical speculation; that we cannot draw an
indictment against a whole people, that there is a species
of hostile justice which no asperity of war wholly extin-
guishes in the minds of a civilized people. " Steady independent minds " he had once said, " when they have an

object of so serious a concern to mankind as *government*
under their contemplation, will disdain to assume the part
of satirists and declaimers." Show the thing that you ask
for, he cried during the American war, to be reason, show
it to be common-sense. We have a measure of the reason and common-sense of Burke's attitude in the *Regicide
Peace*, in the language which it inspired in Windham and
others, who denounce Wilberforce for canting when he
spoke of peace ; who stigmatized Pitt as weak, and a pan-
der to national avarice for thinking of the cost of the war;
and who actually charged the liverymen of London who
petitioned for peace, with open sedition.

It is a striking illustration of the versatility of Burke's
moods, that immediately before sitting down to write the
flaming *Letters on a Regicide Peace*, he had composed one
of the most lucid and accurately meditated of all his tracts,
which, short as it is, contains ideas on free trade which
was only too far in advance of the opinion of his time.
In 1772 a Corn Bill had been introduced—it was passed
in the following year—of which Adam Smith said, that
it was like the laws of Solon, not the best in itself, but
the best which the situation and tendency of the times
would admit. In speaking upon this measure, Burke had
laid down those sensible principles on the trade in corn,
which he now in 1795 worked out in the *Thoughts and
Details on Scarcity*. Those who do not concern themselves with economics will perhaps be interested in the
singular passage, vigorously objected to by Dugald Stewart, in which Burke sets up a genial defence of the con-
sumption of ardent spirits. It is interesting as an argument, and it is most characteristic of the author.

The curtain was now falling. All who saw him, felt
that Burke's life was quickly drawing to a close. His

son's death had struck the final blow. We could only
wish that the years had brought to him, what it ought to
be the fervent prayer of us all to find at the close of the
long struggle with ourselves and with circumstance — a
disposition to happiness, a composed spirit to which time
has made things clear, an unrebellious temper, and hopes
undimmed for mankind. If this was not so, Burke at
least busied himself to the end in great interests. His
charity to the unfortunate emigrants from France was diligent and unwearied. Among other solid services, he established a school at Beaconsfield for sixty French boys,
principally the orphans of Quiberon, and the children of
other emigrants who had suffered in the cause. Almost
the last glimpse that we have of Burke is in a record of
a visit to Beaconsfield by the author of the *Vindiciæ Gallicæ*. Mackintosh had written to Burke to express his admiration for his character and genius, and recanting his old
defence of the Revolution. "Since that time," he said, " a
melancholy experience has undeceived me on many subjects, in which I was then the dupe of my enthusiasm."
When Mackintosh went to Beaconsfield (Christmas, 1797),
he was as much amazed as every one else with the exuber-
ance of his host's mind in conversation. Even then Burke
entered with cordial glee into the sports of children, roll-
ing about with them on the carpet, and pouring out in
his gambols the sublimest images, mixed with the most
wretched puns. He said of Fox, with a deep sigh, " He
is made to be loved." There was the irresistible outbreak
against "that putrid carcase, that mother of all evil—the
French Revolution." It reminded him of the accursed
things that crawled in and out of the mouth of the vile
hag in Spenser's Cave of Error ; and he repeated the nau-
seous stanza. Mackintosh was to be the faithful knight

of the romance, the brightness of whose sword was to flash destruction on the filthy progeny.

It was on the 9th of July, 1797, that in the sixty-eighth year of his age, preserving his faculties to the last moment, he expired. With magnanimous tenderness, Fox proposed that he should be buried among the great dead in Westminster Abbey ; but Burke had left strict injunctions that his funeral should be private, and he was laid in the little church at Beaconsfield. It was a terrible moment in the history of England and of Europe. An open mutiny had just been quelled in the fleet. There had been signs of disaffection in the army. In Ireland the spirit of revolt was smouldering, which in a few months broke out in the fierce flames of a great rebellion. And it was the year of the political crime of Campo Formio, that sinister pacification in which violence and fraud once more asserted their unveiled ascendancy in Europe. These sombre shadows were falling over the western world, when a life went out, which, notwithstanding some grave aberrations, had made great tides in human destiny very luminous.

CHAPTER X.

A STORY is told that in the time when Burke was still at peace with the Dissenters, he visited Priestley, and after seeing his library and his laboratory, and hearing how his host's hours were given to experiment and meditation, he exclaimed that such a life must make him the happiest and most to be envied of men. It must sometimes have occurred to Burke to wonder whether he had made the right choice when he locked away the fragments of his history, and plunged into the torment of party and Parliament. But his interests and aptitudes were too strong and overmastering for him to have been right in doing otherwise. Contact with affairs was an indispensable condition for the full use of his great faculties, in spite of their being less faculties of affairs than of speculation. Public life was the actual field in which to test, and work out, and use with good effect the moral ideas which were Burke's most sincere and genuine interests. And he was able to bring these moral ideas into such effective use because he was so entirely unfettered by the narrowing spirit of formula. No man, for instance, who thought in formulæ would have written the curious passage that I have already referred to, in which he eulogises gin, because " under the pressure of the cares and sorrows of our mortal condition, men have at all times and in all countries

called in some physical aid to their moral consolation."
He valued words at their proper rate; that is to say, he
knew that some of the greatest facts in the life and character of man, and in the institutions of society, can find
no description and no measurement in words. Public life,
as we can easily perceive, with its shibboleths, its exclusive parties, its measurement by conventional standards, its
attention to small expediencies before the larger ones, is
not a field where such characteristics are likely to make
an instant effect.

Though it is not wrong to say of Burke that, as an orator, he was transcendent, yet in that immediate influence
upon his hearers which is commonly supposed to be the
mark of oratorical success, all the evidence is that Burke
generally failed. We have seen how his speech against
Hastings affected Miss Burney, and how the speech on
the Nabob of Arcot's debts was judged by Pitt not to be
worth answering. Perhaps the greatest that he ever made
was that on conciliation with America; the wisest in its
temper, the most closely logical in its reasoning, the am-
plest in appropriate topics, the most generous and conciliatory in the substance of its appeals. Yet Erskine, who
was in the House when this was delivered, said that it
drove everybody away, including people who, when they
came to read it, read it over and over again, and could
hardly think of anything else. As Moore says rather too
floridly, but with truth—" In vain did Burke's genius put
forth its superb plumage, glittering all over with the hundred eyes of fancy—the gait of the bird was heavy and
awkward, and its voice seemed rather to scare than attract."
Burke's gestures were clumsy; he had sonorous but harsh
tones; he never lost a strong Irish accent; and his utter-
ance was often hurried and eager. Apart from these dis-

advantages of accident which have been overcome by men
infinitely inferior to Burke, it is easy to perceive, from the
matter and texture of the speeches that have become English classics, that the very qualities which are excellences
in literature were drawbacks to the spoken discourses. A
listener in Westminster Hall or the House of Commons,
unlike the reader by his fireside in the next century, is always thinking of arguments and facts that bear directly
on the special issue before him. What he wishes to hear
is some particularity of event or inference which will either help him to make up his mind, or will justify him if
his mind is already made up. Burke never neglected these
particularities, and he never went so wide as to fall for an
instant into vagueness, but he went wide enough into the
generalities that lent force and light to his view, to weary
men who cared for nothing, and could not be expected to
care for anything, but the business actually in hand and
the most expeditious way through it. The contentious-
ness is not close enough and rapid enough to hold the interest of a practical assembly, which, though it was a hundred times less busy than the House of Commons to-day,
seems to have been eager in the inverse proportion of what
it had to do, to get that little quickly done.

Then we may doubt whether there is any instance of
an orator throwing his spell over a large audience, without
frequent resort to the higher forms of commonplace. Two
of the greatest speeches of Burke's time are supposed to
have been Grattan's on Tithes and Fox's on the Westminster Scrutiny, and these were evidently full of the splendid
commonplaces of the first-rate rhetorician. Burke's mind
was not readily set to these tunes. The emotion to which
he commonly appealed was that too rare one, the love of
wisdom; and he combined his thoughts and knowledge in

propositions of wisdom so weighty and strong, that the minds of ordinary hearers were not on the instant prepared for them.

It is true that Burke's speeches were not without effect of an indirect kind, for there is good evidence that at the time when Lord North's ministry was tottering, Burke had risen to a position of the first eminence in Parliament. When Boswell said to him that people would wonder how he could bring himself to take so much pains with his speeches, knowing with certainty that not one vote would be gained by them, Burke answered that it is very well worth while to take pains to speak well in Parliament; for if a man speaks well, he gradually establishes a certain reputation and consequence in the general opinion; and though an Act that has been ably opposed becomes law, yet in its progress it is softened and modified to meet objections whose force has never been acknowledged directly. "Aye, sir," Johnson broke in, "and there is a gratification of pride. Though we cannot out-vote them, we will out-argue them."

Out-arguing is not perhaps the right word for most of Burke's performances. He is at heart thinking more of the subject itself than of those on whom it was his apparent business to impress a particular view of it. He surrenders himself wholly to the matter, and follows up, though with a strong and close tread, all the excursions to which it may give rise in an elastic intelligence—"motion," as De Quincey says, "propagating motion, and life throwing off life." But then this exuberant way of thinking, this willingness to let the subject lead, is less apt in public discourse than it is in literature, and from this comes the literary quality of Burke's speeches.

With all his hatred for the book-man in politics, Burke

owed much of his own distinction to that generous rich-
ness and breadth of judgment which had been ripened in
him by literature and his practice in it. Like some other
men in our history, he showed that books are a better
preparation for statesmanship than early training in the
subordinate posts and among the permanent officials of a
public department. There is no copiousness of literary
reference in his works, such as over-abounded in civil and
ecclesiastical publicists of the seventeenth century. Nor
can we truly say that there is much, though there is certainly some, of that tact which literature is alleged to confer on those who approach it in a just spirit and with the
true gift. The influence of literature on Burke lay partly
in the direction of emancipation from the mechanical formulæ of practical politics; partly in the association which
it engendered, in a powerful understanding like his, between politics and the moral forces of the world, and between political maxims and the old and great sentences of
morals; partly in drawing him, even when resting his case
on prudence and expediency, to appeal to the widest and
highest sympathies; partly, and more than all, in opening
his thoughts to the many conditions, possibilities, and " varieties of untried being " in human character and situation,
and so giving an incomparable flexibility to his methods
of political approach.

This flexibility is not to be found in his manner and
composition. That derives its immense power from other
sources; from passion, intensity, imagination, size, truth,
cogency of logical reason. If any one has imbued himself
with that exacting love of delicacy, measure, and taste in
expression, which was until our own day a sacred tradition
of the French, then he will not like Burke. Those who insist on charm, on winningness in style, on subtle harmonies

10

and exquisite suggestion, are disappointed in Burke; they
even find him stiff and over-coloured. And there are
blemishes of this kind. His banter is nearly always un-
gainly, his wit blunt, as Johnson said of it, and very often
unseasonable. We feel that Johnson must have been right
in declaring that though Burke was always in search of
pleasantries, he never made a good joke in his life. As is
usual with a man who has not true humour, Burke is also
without true pathos. The thought of wrong or misery
moved him less to pity for the victim than to anger against
the cause. Again, there are some gratuitous and unre-
deemed vulgarities; some images whose barbarity makes
us shudder, of creeping ascarides and inexpugnable tape-
worms. But it is the mere foppery of literature to suffer
ourselves to be long detained by specks like these.

The varieties of Burke's literary or rhetorical method
are very striking. It is almost incredible that the superb
imaginative amplification of the description of Hyder Ali's
descent upon the Carnatic should be from the same pen as
the grave, simple, unadorned *Address to the King* (1777),
where each sentence falls on the ear with the accent of
some golden-tongued oracle of the wise gods. His stride
is the stride of a giant, from the sentimental beauty of the
picture of Marie Antoinette at Versailles, or the red horror
of the tale of Debi Sing in Rungpore, to the learning, pos-
itiveness, and cool judicial mastery of the *Report on the
Lords' Journals* (1794), which Philip Francis, no mean
judge, declared on the whole to be the " most eminent and
extraordinary " of all his productions. Even in the cool-
est and dryest of his pieces there is the mark of greatness,
of grasp, of comprehension. In all its varieties Burke's
style is noble, earnest, deep-flowing, because his sentiment
was lofty and fervid, and went with sincerity and ardent

disciplined travail of judgment. Fox told Francis Horner that Dryden's prose was Burke's great favourite, and that Burke imitated him more than anyone else. We may well believe that he was attracted by Dryden's ease, his copiousness, his gaiety, his manliness of style, but there can hardly have been any conscious attempt at imitation. Their topics were too different. Burke had the style of his subjects, the amplitude, the weightiness, the laboriousness, the sense, the high flight, the grandeur, proper to a man dealing with imperial themes, the freedom of nations, the justice of rulers, the fortunes of great societies, the sacredness of law. Burke will always be read with delight and edification, because in the midst of discussions on the local and the accidental, he scatters apophthegms that take us into the regions of lasting wisdom. In the midst of the torrent of his most strenuous and passionate deliverances, he suddenly rises aloof from his immediate subject, and in all tranquillity reminds us of some permanent relation of things, some enduring truth of human life or society. We do not hear the organ tones of Milton, for faith and freedom had other notes in the seventeenth century. There is none of the complacent and wise-browed sagacity of Bacon, for Burke's were days of eager personal strife and party fire and civil division. We are not exhilarated by the cheerfulness, the polish, the fine manners of Bolingbroke, for Burke had an anxious conscience, and was earnest and intent that the good should triumph. And yet Burke is among the greatest of those who have wrought marvels in the prose of our English tongue.

The influence of Burke on the publicists of the generation after the Revolution was much less considerable than might have been expected. In Germany, where there has been so much excellent writing about *Staatswissenschaft*,

with such poverty and darkness in the wisdom of practical politics, there is a long list of writers who have drawn
their inspiration from Burke.   In France, publicists of the
sentimental school, like Chateaubriand, and the politico-
ecclesiastical school, like De Maistre, fashioned a track of
their own.   In England Burke made a deep mark on contemporary opinion during the last years of his life, and
then his influence underwent a certain eclipse.   The official Whigs considered him a renegade and a heresiarch,
who had committed the deadly sin of breaking up the
party, and they never mentioned his name without bitterness.   To men like Godwin, the author of *Political Justice*, Burke was as antichrist.   Bentham and James Mill
thought of him as a declaimer who lived upon applause,
and who, as one of them says, was for protecting everything old, not because it was good but because it existed.
In one quarter only did he exert a profound influence.
His maxim that men might employ their sagacity in dis-
covering the latent wisdom which underlies general prejudices and old institutions, instead of exploding them, inspired Coleridge, as I have already said; and the Coleridg-
ian school are Burke's direct descendants, whenever they
deal with the significance and the relations of Church and
State.   But they connected these views so closely with
their views in metaphysics and theology, that the association with Burke was effectually disguised.

The only English writer of that age whom we can name
along with Burke in the literature of enduring power, is
Wordsworth, that great representative in another and a
higher field, and with many rare elements added that were
all his own, of those harmonizing and conciliatory forces
and ideas that make man's destiny easier to him through
piety in its oldest and best sense; through reverence for

the past, for duty, for institutions. He was born in the
year of the *Present Discontents* (1770) ; and when Burke
wrote the *Reflections*, Wordsworth was standing, with
France "on the top of golden hours," listening with delight among the ruins of the Bastille, or on the banks of
the Loire, to "the homeless sound of joy that was in the
sky." When France lost faith and freedom, and Napoleon
had built his throne on their grave, he began to see those
strong elements which for Burke had all his life been the
true and fast foundation of the social world. Wide as is
the difference between an oratorical and a declamatory
mind like Burke's, and the least oratorical of all poets, yet,
under this difference of form and temper, there is a striking likeness in spirit. There was the same energetic feeling about moral ideas, the same frame of counsel and
prudence, the same love for the slowness of time, the same
slight account held of mere intellectual knowledge, and
even the same ruling sympathy with that side of the character of Englishmen which Burke exulted in, as " *their awe
of kings and reverence for priests*," " *their sullen resistance
of innovation*," "*their unalterable perseverance in the wisdom of prejudice*."

The conservative movement in England ran on for many
years in the ecclesiastical channel, rather than among questions where Burke's writings might have been brought to
bear. On the political side the most active minds, both
in practice and theory, worked out the principles of liberalism, and they did so on a plan and by methods from
which Burke's utilitarian liberalism and his historic conservatism were equally remote. There are many signs
around us that this epoch is for the moment at an end.
The historic method, fitting in with certain dominant con-
ceptions in the region of natural science, is bringing men

round to a way of looking at society for which Burke's maxims are exactly suited; and it seems probable that he will be more frequently and more seriously referred to within the next twenty years than he has been within the whole of the last eighty.

THE END.

ENGLISH MEN OF LETTERS.

EDITED BY JOHN MORLEY.

12mo, Cloth, 75 cents per Volume.

Others will be announced.

PUBLISHED BY HARPER & BROTHERS, NEW YORK.

☞ Harper & Brothers *will send any of the above works by mail, postage prepaid, to any part of the United States, on receipt of the price.*

A NEW LIBRARY EDITION

OF

MACAULAY'S ENGLAND.

MACAULAY'S HISTORY OF ENGLAND. New Edition, from New Electrotype Plates. 5 volumes, 8vo, Cloth, with Paper Labels, Gilt Tops and Uncut Edges, $10 00; Sheep, $12 50; Half Calf, $21 25. *Sold only in Sets.*

The beauty of the edition is the beauty of proper workmanship and solid worth—the beauty of fitness alone. Nowhere is the least effort made to decorate the volumes externally or internally. They are perfectly printed from new plates that have been made in the best manner, and with the most accurate understanding of what is needed; and they are solidly bound, with absolutely plain black cloth covers, without relief of any kind, except such as is afforded by the paper label. It is a set of plain, solid, sensible volumes, made for use, and so made as to be comfortable] in the using.— *N. Y. Evening Post.*

OTHER EDITIONS OF MACAULAY'S ENGLAND.

LIBRARY EDITION: 5 volumes, 8vo, Cloth, $10 00.

POPULAR EDITION: 5 volumes, 12mo, Cloth, $2 50.

CHEAP EDITION: 5 volumes, 8vo, Paper, $1 00, In one volume, 8vo, Cloth, $1 25.

The volumes are sold separately.

Published by **HARPER & BROTHERS**, New York.

☞ *Sent by mail, postage prepaid, to any part of the United States, on receipt of the price.*

OLIVER GOLDSMITH.

POETICAL WORKS OF OLIVER GOLDSMITH.

With a Biographical Memoir, and Notes on the Poems. **Edited** by BOLTON CORNEY. Illustrated. 8vo, Cloth, $3 00; Cloth, **Gilt** Edges, $3 75; Turkey Morocco, Gilt Edges, $7 50.

SELECT POEMS OF OLIVER GOLDSMITH.

Edited, with Notes, by WILLIAM J. ROLFE, A.M. Illustrated. Small 4to, Flexible Cloth, 70 cents; Paper, 50 cents.

GOLDSMITH'S POEMS.

32mo, Paper, 25 cents; Cloth, 40 cents.

GOLDSMITH'S PLAYS.

32mo, Paper, 20 cents; Cloth, 35 cents.

THE VICAR OF WAKEFIELD.

By OLIVER GOLDSMITH. 18mo, Cloth, 50 cents. 32mo, **Paper,** 25 cents; Cloth, 40 cents.

GOLDSMITH. By WILLIAM BLACK.

Goldsmith. By WILLIAM BLACK. A Critical and Biographical Sketch. (In the series entitled "English Men of Letters.") 12mo, Cloth, 75 cents.

GOLDSMITH.—BUNYAN.—MADAME D'ARBLAY.

By LORD MACAULAY. 32mo, Paper, 25 cents; Cloth, 40 **cents.**

HISTORY OF GREECE.

By OLIVER GOLDSMITH. Abridged by the Author. 18mo, Cloth, 75 cents.

HISTORY OF ROME.

By OLIVER GOLDSMITH. Abridged by the Author. 18mo, Cloth, 75 cents.

OLIVER GOLDSMITH. By WASHINGTON IRVING.

Life of Oliver Goldsmith. With Selections from his Writings. By WASHINGTON IRVING. 2 vols., 18mo, Cloth, $1 50.

Published by HARPER & BROTHERS, New York.

☞ *Any of the above works will be sent by mail, postage prepaid, to any part of the United States, on receipt of the price.*

MOTLEY'S HISTORIES.

CHEAP EDITION.

THE RISE OF THE DUTCH REPUBLIC. A History. By JOHN LOTHROP MOTLEY, LL.D., D.C.L. With a Portrait of William of Orange. 3 volumes, 8vo, Cloth with Paper Labels, Uncut Edges and Gilt Tops, $6 00. *Sold only in Sets.*

HISTORY OF THE UNITED NETHERLANDS: from the Death of William the Silent to the Twelve-Years' Truce. With a full View of the English-Dutch Struggle against Spain, and of the Origin and Destruction of the Spanish Armada. By JOHN LOTHROP MOTLEY, LL.D., D.C.L. With Portraits. 4 volumes, 8vo, Cloth with Paper Labels, Uncut Edges and Gilt Tops, $8 00. *Sold only in Sets.*

LIFE AND DEATH OF JOHN OF BARNEVELD, Advocate of Holland. With a View of the Primary Causes and Movements of the "Thirty-Years' War." By JOHN LOTHROP MOTLEY, LL.D., D.C.L. Illustrated. 2 volumes, 8vo, Cloth with Paper Labels, Uncut Edges and Gilt Tops, $4 00. *Sold only in Sets.*

This edition of Motley's "Complete Historical Works" affords an opportunity to the collector of choice standard works to fill a possible vacancy in his library at a moderate cost. The reader of Motley always returns to the perusal of his writings with a zest which may be compared to the taste of the ripe strawberries in early June. The freshness of his mind never fails to give a flavor to his narrative. His descriptions read less like a recital of the faded past than a vivid picture of living scenes. No historian transports so much of himself into his writings; and though without the faintest trace of egotism, they are always intensely human and individual.—*N.Y. Tribune.*

The original Library Edition, on larger paper, of Mr. Motley's Histories can still be supplied: "The Dutch Republic," 3 vols.; "The History of the United Netherlands," 4 vols.; "Life and Death of John of Barneveld," 2 vols. Price *per volume*, in Cloth, $3 50; in Sheep, $4 00; in Half Calf or Half Morocco, $5 75. *The volumes of this original edition sold separately.*

Published by HARPER & BROTHERS, New York.

☞ *Sent by mail, postage prepaid, to any part of the United States, on receipt of the price.*

SAMUEL JOHNSON.

BOSWELL'S JOHNSON.

The Life of Samuel Johnson, LL.D. Including a Journal of a Tour to the Hebrides. By JAMES BOSWELL, Esq. Portrait of Boswell. 2 vols., 8vo, Cloth, $4 00; Sheep, $5 00; Half Calf, $8 50.

JOHNSON'S WORKS.

The Complete Works of Samuel Johnson, LL.D. With an Essay on his Life and Genius, by ARTHUR MURPHY, Esq. 2 vols., 8vo, Cloth, $4 00; Sheep, $5 00; Half Calf, $8 50.

SAMUEL JOHNSON. By LESLIE STEPHEN.

Samuel Johnson. By LESLIE STEPHEN. A Critical and Biographical Sketch. (In the series entitled "English Men of Letters.") 12mo, Cloth, 75 cents.

JOHNSON'S LIFE AND WRITINGS.

Selected and Arranged by the Rev. WILLIAM P. PAGE. 2 vols., 18mo, Cloth, $1 50.

JOHNSON. By Lord MACAULAY.

Samuel Johnson, LL.D. By Lord MACAULAY. 32mo, Paper, 25 cents.

JOHNSON'S RELIGIOUS LIFE.

The Religious Life and Death of Dr. Johnson. 12mo, Cloth, $1 50.

SAMUEL JOHNSON. By E. T. MASON.

Samuel Johnson: His Words and his Ways; What he Said, What he Did, and What Men Thought and Spoke Concerning Him. Edited by E. T. MASON. 12mo, Cloth, $1 50.

Published by HARPER & BROTHERS, New York.

☞ *Any of the above works will be sent by mail, postage prepaid, to any part of the United States, on receipt of the price.*